THE
MIND
BENDERS

When Longman went into the Tank he wanted to prove that extended submersion in a limbo of sightless, soundless isolation could corrode a man's personality, change his most fundamental convictions.

Days after his ordeal, Longman seemed to be unaffected, and the experiment a failure. At first it was only his wife who noticed a difference. Her husband's passionate ardor had become hatred. Even her slightest touch seemed to arouse his revulsion . . .

The destruction of a man's love for his wife and family, and a stunning glimpse into current experimental work in the field of human isolation is the basis for this fascinating and unforgettable novel.

"Mr. Kennaway's treatment of this nightmare and his horrifying suggestions of other methods for bending minds makes this a first-rate thriller . . . an excellent novel of suspense."—

—LONDON TIMES LITERARY SUPPLEMENT

"It belongs to the same literary genre as *Fail-Safe* and *Seven Days in May*."

—LOUISVILLE COURIER-JOURNAL

James Kennaway

THE
MIND
BENDERS

A SIGNET BOOK
Published by The New American Library

Published as a SIGNET BOOK
by arrangement with Atheneum Publishers,
who have authorized this softcover edition.
A hardcover edition is available from Atheneum Publishers.

First Printing, September, 1964

SIGNET TRADEMARK REG. U.S. PAT. OFF. AND FOREIGN COUNTRIES
REGISTERED TRADEMARK—MARCA REGISTRADA
HECHO EN CHICAGO, U.S.A.

SIGNET BOOKS are published by
The New American Library of World Literature, Inc.
501 Madison Avenue, New York, New York 10022

PRINTED IN THE UNITED STATES OF AMERICA

for E R I C, MY STEP-FATHER

and E R I C, MY FATHER-IN-LAW

Publisher's Note

This story was suggested by experiments on the Reduction of Sensation recently carried out at McGill University in Canada, at the University of Indiana, and other Universities in the United States.
While making this acknowledgment, the publishers and author wish to emphasize that the events and characters are fictitious. Any similarity to actual events or persons, living or dead, is purely coincidental.

PART ONE

1

Major Hall, let's face it, was hardly as exciting as his celebrated colleague in Military Intelligence, James Bond. But then the personnel of the counter-espionage department, MI5, tend to be more conservative, and even in Curzon Street, where old soldiers turn to Intelligence, Hall was considered something of a joke with his ramrod figure and his ramrod principles. It was hard to decide which was the outstanding characteristic; the squareness of his personality or the narrowness of his outlook. It did not, however, occur to his colleagues, even those from cavalry regiments, that only nervous beasts need blinkers. Ramrod Hall, it was supposed, had no soul.

He was certainly lamentably short on imagination, but this was perhaps an asset in his job. As he stood at the end of the library in Albemarle Street, pretending to be engrossed in Partington's *Advanced Treatise on Physical Chemistry,* Vol. 4, he was reconsidering the man he was shadowing in plodding, military manner. He did so absolutely according to the book, heading his thoughts, logically and unemotionally:

Re-appreciation of Prof. Sharpey. (1) Factors:-

Ground. The library of the Royal Institution of Great Britain, Albemarle Street, W1, on a wet Spring afternoon, 1604 hours.

Enemy troops. Professor S. V. Sharpey, Oxford Biologist, aged 67, Nobel Prize Winner, gentleman of good family, leftish views, sitting huddled over a table at far end of elegant eighteenth-century room.

The Professor has visited London at least once a week and sometimes twice, consorting with people defined as undesirable, three from foreign embassies, one from a Continental publishing house in whose activities the Department is already interested. The Professor has access to various Classified fields of Research in the biological sciences, including biological warfare and space physiology. On the other hand, in spite of loudly and naïvely expressed political views of a socialistic order his previous record, since and especially during the war, is clean. His reputation has been that of a balanced, loyal Briton. The Professor does not appear to be in debt, according to Departmental inquiry, and there is no question of homosexuality or any other immoral practice which could make him the easy target of blackmailers. The Professor does not seem to be enjoying the best of health. . . .

For a moment, then, the grinding wheel of methodical military intelligence was halted. The Professor at the far end of the room shifted in his chair and began very slowly to extract from a brief-case, as old and battered as a school leaver's music case, several objects or packages. Our man Ramrod instructed himself to take two short paces to the left, and instantly obeyed himself, but to no consequence as he was still unable to see the objects now lying on the table in front of the old man. After another quick appreciation of this new and challenging situation he decided against further advance. A couple of yards away from the shelves, he felt almost as conspicuous as he looked. The consideration that the Professor did not appear to be in the best of health was the military understatement of the week. The old man looked sadder than his big, drooping moustache. His grey hairs seemed to be dragging him swiftly to his grave. He was listless, dazed, and infinitely weary.

Turning over another indecipherable page of the advanced treatise on a subject which he had not considered since pre-Camberly days, Ramrod doggedly returned to his general appreciation of the situation, picking it up at point number two - *object*. This was easily answered. Nine times out of ten, in his work, the object was the same, namely to ascertain whether the subject under examination was a threat to her majesty and her commonwealth.

(3) *Courses open*. Ramrod never departed from the formula he had learnt as a cadet in the first lecture laying down the rules of how to think. He subdivided *Courses open,* then, as follows:

(1) Follow the blighter until he gets on to the Oxford train then report back that this foreign publisher lunched him again.

(2) Slip downstairs and report back, immediately, demanding further instructions.

(3) Assume that the old man will as usual head for the five-fifty - correctly 1750 hours - express train back to Oxford, and proceed straightway to the In and Out club for tea and buns.

He was now heading dangerously close to the paragraph entitled *Conclusion,* and therefore continued to rack his brain for more courses open, an operation which he accomplished about as deftly as a five-year-old dealing out cards. The lethargic process was however cut short again by a movement on the Professor's part.

The old man sighed, a sigh with a waist to it, a plaintiff world-weary double sigh, then slowly, as if in a dream, began to collect the little packages together again. As he did so, he leant back slightly, unconcerned apparently whether anybody should see what he was doing.

Daringly, Ramrod took two or three paces forward
then halted, blushed, and retired four. He realized that
the whole situation had changed since the formulation
of his appreciation, and now swiftly reappreciated. There
was a new, startling factor. The old man's brief-case
was stuffed with fivers. The packages were all the same,
containing fifty five pound notes each.

A moment later the Professor rose, stiffly, closed his
brief-case, and very slowly moved to the far doors of
the library. Ramrod, with care, replaced the treatise
in its correct position, aligned it with its neighbouring
volumes, and set out in pursuit. The new factor had
much bearing on the expressed object. The conclusion
was clear. He would follow the Professor not only
to the Oxford train, but to Didcot and stations beyond,
all the way to Oxford itself, and he would not let the
old man out of his sight. He would forego tea and buns
and hope to ring back to Headquarters at the station.
In the meantime, the Professor was winding down the
stairs with the marble bannister and proceeding to the
big front doors. One of the porters hailed him a taxi,
for Paddington.

Ramrod Hall put his felt hat firmly on his head, brim
well over the eyes. He too hailed a taxi.

"Paddington - the Railway Station," he said.

"No —" the cabbie said in mock surprise. "I thought
that was an helicopter port, these days."

Ramrod Hall was baffled, always, by irony. He said,
"I believe if you follow that cab in front he will lead
us to our destination," then he sat back, opened *The
Times,* and read about dead friends.

Ramrod Hall, had he been asked at this stage about
the sorts of traitor there can be would have denied the
possibility of such a question. All men were traitors
or patriots, as all eggs are good or bad. There was
nothing of the curate about Ramrod.

2

There was, however, much of the curate in Jack Tate. Eggs for him were neither good nor bad, but more or less sulphuric. He was not the man to muddle qualitative terms with measurable conditions. For Tate was a don; a young don; a nice young don; a nice, frustrated young don - frustrated, in fact, for a score of reasons, but at five forty-five, at Paddington this afternoon, he was particularly frustrated because there was no sign of the Professor. The train was already crowded. It would be impossible to hang on to the window seats much longer.

Tate wandered round in little circles, outside the compartment door, as people streamed past him. Paddington, like the egg, seemed more or less sulphuric, and this gloomy afternoon it was at its worst. Not all the bright ideas, the new lettering on the boards, the new shops and refreshment stalls and coloured posters - none of these things could disguise the essential, apprehensive quality of the departure platforms. Banging his open palm with a rolled newspaper, Tate fought wave after wave of *Angst,* wondering what could have happened to the old man.

Around him, there were the usual, bald and baring good-byes; parents staring blankly at pimply sons, and middle-aged lovers arguing. Very close, there was one of these debutante undergraduates, a girl who had succeeded in adopting the worst characteristics of both her worlds. She was dressed unerotically, like an overgrown school girl, but the voice was straight from a Queen Charlotte's ball, or a Douglas-Home play. The language had already been affected by some weeks at Oxford.

"But darling," she was telling her plain friend, "you don't realize - everybody's being foul to me. I mean one's parents are so unclear. Do they want one to get a first-class degree or a first-class husband? One simply can't get both. Even if one had the talent, any ass can see that the two are mutually exclusive. Any ass, that is," she added with a peal of laughter that rang down the platform "except mummy —" And "mummy" sounded like "mubby".

Tate stared at her with solemn hatred, telling himself that he should not judge so hastily. He was aware that his nerves were a little frayed; the winter had seemed interminable and the new teaching term which led up to the most important exams had only just begun. The minute hand of the huge clock moved on. He circled again, frowning more deeply. The Professor was quite capable of getting himself run over by a bus. That was the traditional fate of absent-minded professors, and in the past few weeks he had been quite out of touch with the world round about him. On the journey up to town that morning he had not uttered a word, but had sat with his head slightly on one side, as if he were a kind of exhausted Prospero, abandoned by both Ariel and Caliban, listening to distant music, reminded perhaps, of some Miranda that had gone. Tate knew that the debutante's voice would do nothing to soothe him, so he turned away and walked a few paces in the opposite direction.

There he was faced with another dreadful good-bye scene. A son in a scarf was lecturing a father with a pot and a sad, cheery looking mum with pot-hat. The boy had a pronounced *nouvelle vague* accent which, in its way, was equally as affected as the debutante's.

"No," he was saying, like a Nottingham donkey. "Noa . . . Don't get me wrong, Dad. Don't take me like that. 'Course I enjoyed it. I wouldn't 've chosen it, myself, but that's not the point. 'Course I enjoyed it, but I mean, look at that title—'My fair lady'—After all, Shaw wasn't that kind of writer, was he? I mean he didn't skip issues —"

"You will get your hair cut, Tom, won't you?" his mother asked sadly, by way of socratic reply, and the boy groaned.

But then, at last, as he turned back, Tate spotted the Professor coming trailing down the platform. At once, he went to meet him. The Professor had looked vague enough this morning, but never as sad and exhausted as this. Tate called out, waved his paper, calling, "Professor! Professor Sharpey?" But he had to repeat himself several times before the old man recognized him. He seemed to be awoken from a bad dream. He stood, his weight on his heels, apologizing for not having answered his assistant at once. Tate asked him, then, "You're all right?"

Sharpey seemed to be a little better.

"Yes, oh yes. Perfectly." Then it was as if his mind were slipping away again. "I . . ."

"You're sure?" Tate asked.

"I . . ." But Sharpey seemed to lose track of what he had been going to say. As Tate took his arm and walked towards their compartment the loudspeaker boomed out the final notice. "The train now leaving from Platform 7 is the five-fifty for Reading, Didcot, and Oxford. Passengers for Swindon, Cirencester . . ." The voice was lost in a hiss of steam. As he climbed into the train Sharpey tried to recover himself again. He said, "Thank you, Tate, yes . . . yes. London is very tiring." He looked around the crowded little compartment as if it were a prison cell. He said as much to the other passengers as to Tate, "I'm just a little tired." Then he gave another deep sigh which seemed to shake him to the spine. Tate had to touch his sleeve to remind him to sit down. The old man did so obediently, at last, like a schoolboy, and again like the schoolboy, did not bother to unbutton his overcoat. He sat upright and stiffly, with his brief-case like a satchel on his knees, and he stared vaguely out of the window as if all the world were at war.

Tate, in spite of his anxieties and frustration, looked solid enough. He was not particularly good looking, but he had an honest face. The sort of face, he described it, himself, that people want to lean on. So when the old lady opposite dropped her magazine she seemed pleased but not surprised that Tate picked it up. But Tate had made friends and influenced nobody too easily for too long. He was sharply observant, and spotting that the magazine was *The Nursery World* he calculated that the lady was a Superannuated Nanny, and very quickly opened up his own evening paper, and hid behind it. The old lady tipped forward and tapped his knee.

She said, "I wonder if you're thinking, 'Why should an old lady like that be reading the Nursery World?' "

Tate looked trapped. He blushed and smiled.

"I am not a grandmother," she said, and with a little giggle went on, "I should hope not. I am not married. . . . I'll tell you." Tate nodded.

She said, in a whisper as if passing a state secret, "I was a Nanny." She sat back. "Oh yes, I was."

Tate knew that one word would invite a thousand. He let the smile freeze, in a glazed kind of way, on his face, then picked up his paper again. The old lady sat and stared at his shoes, doubtless plotting some new line of attack.

Two Indian students, Hindus of indeterminate age, were sitting in the inside seats of the compartment. Abruptly, about half an hour later, one of these broke the silence again. Speaking swiftly and extremely loudly he said, "There is an apocryphal story that the famous Doctor Einstein, travelling on exactly this train route, before the publication of his celebrated Relativity theory, is asking 'Does Oxford stop at this train?' " For a moment his companion did not seem to understand. The first one underlined the joke. He said, "I find this an exceptionally amusing anecdote," and at last the other began to giggle rather girlishly, nodding his head, saying, "Oh yes, very amusing. Very, very good."

There was a pause. Tate did not dare move his paper for fear of catching their eyes, or the Nanny's. Then very loudly again, the Indian continued, "I am thinking what is particularly significant about this anecdote, which might perhaps be better described as a philosopher's chestnut, is that the incident is assumed to have taken place in circumstances that —"

But he never finished.

It happened, so it seemed to Tate, in a slow motion flash. It was all over, that is to say, before anybody had time to move, yet, in contradiction to time, no detail was missed by any of the other occupants of the compartment.

Sharpey's eyes had been closed for some moments. He opened them, seemed absolutely, suddenly wide awake and aware of what he was doing. It was almost dark outside. His collar looked soft and white, peeping above his great-coat. He stood up, holding the brief-case, and the others moved back their feet to allow him room to pass through to the corridor. But he chose the other door. There was a very loud "crack" as the door swung back, and the noise of the wheels passing over the joins in the rail filled the compartment. Then, paradoxically again, in complete silence and slow motion, in the shape of a star, the old man floated through the door, to land face down on the cinder track outside. Everybody rose to their feet.

Reality returned. The train which must have been travelling at seventy miles an hour swung and lurched, and Tate had to hang on to the luggage rack as he reached forward to pull the emergency cord. A loop of the little chain came rattling down and streamed out of the window as the noise of the brakes filled the night. What seemed an age later, they came to a stop.

At once Tate leapt out on to the cinder path at the side of the track, and above all the voices, the screams, and the laughter, he heard the debutante undergraduate crying, "Splendid! Somebody must have pulled the *thing*!"

The inane excited comment rang in his ears as he ran back down the track. The Indian students were following him, one of them shouting "man overboard," and a guard was telling people to remain in their compartments. But Tate paid no heed to him. He ran on until, a hundred yards behind the last compartment, he saw the body, still in the shape of a star, looking less as if he had fallen there, more as if he had been run over; rolled into the cinders. His face was unrecognizable, and it was therefore with relief that Tate, with a hand to the old man's heart, discovered that he had been killed stone dead.

With the guard and the Indian students came a very military looking gentleman, with a straight ramrod figure. Tate, even at that moment, thought him vaguely familiar, then assumed, rightly, that he must have noticed him in the crowd, boarding the train. But he did not know Ramrod's name or occupation. It was just that the face rang some bell.

"Dead?" Ramrod asked.

It was the guard who answered. He did so with a nod that seemed to express anger as much as sorrow.

"Why do it this way?" he asked himself out loud. There was a great deal of blood about. Then he asked Ramrod, "Did you know him?" Ramrod half turned towards Tate, who was rubbing some blood off his coat. He told the guard, "It's Professor Sharpey" and even the guard had heard of him. The Indians were excited by the information, they passed it back to other spectators who had jumped down on the tracks.

Ramrod asked Tate, then, "Were you sitting next to him?" But Tate had a tidy and a careful mind. He had been sitting opposite. Therefore, he shook his head. He saw no reason why he should divulge more information to a stranger who seemed also to be something of a meddler.

The Indians were now excusing themselves, to as large an audience as they could grab. They both looked nervous, as if fearing they might be accused and lynched on the spot. The one with the loud voice said, "We can none of us blame ourselves. This is absolutely certain. We are not culpable, in this sense," while his companion, simultaneously, and about an octave higher, said, "It was the most extraordinary tragedy, you see. He simply gets to his feet and leaps from the compartment. It is right what my colleague is saying. In this sense, we are not culpable."

And it was Ramrod, grave but operational, who stunned the rush of words.

"If you'd be so good as to give your names to the guard, gentlemen." Then he added, "I'll take the names of the others in the compartment."

The guard exchanged a glance with Tate who also looked rather amazed at this assumption of authority. But the guard played carefully. With a glance at Ramrod's boots, he asked, "Are you a Police Officer, sir?" Loudly and clearly Ramrod replied, "Not exactly," and left it at that. But he was distracted then, seeing Tate stoop to pick up a brief-case which had fallen a few feet down the nettly bank. Tate got stung as he retrieved it. He therefore pulled it back rather suddenly, but in the fall the case had sprung open and now its contents were displayed in the half light, among the nettles and the wet grass. All the notes were there, and seeing them Tate turned back at once.

"It's his brief-case," he told Ramrod as non-committally as he could, but the old soldier was not so easily satisfied. He took a pace forward and looked past Tate's shoulder at the packets on the ground.

Tate said, "It appears to be money," as Ramrod stooped down beside him, on one knee, in a loading position. Together they retrieved the notes.

"A great deal of money," Ramrod said, without emotion. Then he stood up again, as Tate collected the last of it. He said, "You'd better give it to the guard."

3

Death in a Company, or an Institution, or a lab, seems to create its own Christmas Day. The Christians are more than ever Christians, the nervous and tearful more nervous and tearful, the industrious escape with industry, the cynics say, "I told you so." There is frost in the air. The most insensitive person walking into Sharpey's lab on the morning following Sharpey's death, would have guessed in half a moment that some tragedy had occurred. And now it is already necessary to suggest that Ramrod was less insensitive than he and his colleagues liked to make out. He approached the swinging doors of the new building with dread. Inside were drawn faces; even, in the case of one of the secretaries, red eyes. There was a sustained bellowing noise of whispers. But above all was that sense of holiness that can't be separated from the sense of loss; a halo round a gap.

Ramrod was very gentle in his approach, entering inconspicuously and moving at once to the porter's cabin. But before he could make his inquiry Sharpey's lab assistant, a bright, fair-haired man called Norman who looked ten years younger, at thirty, left the group at the back of the hall and intercepted.

Norman was one of the new men with a curious inner confidence and outward social abruptness; a technician's strength and a technician's bad manners. Witty enough, he never smiled. But he was quick. He kept both hands in the pockets of his white coat.

"Major Hall?"

"That's very clever of you," Ramrod said, removing the felt hat. Other technicians and students hanging about the wide, light hall turned for a moment, regarding the stranger with casual suspicion.

Norman said, "I don't forget faces. You've been here before."

"On several occasions."

"I suppose you're hunting Calder?"

Calder was the senior lecturer and deputy head of the laboratory, under Sharpey. Norman had guessed right. He led the way up one of those modern staircases which you can see through, there being no back to the steps. Voices carried in the hall and stairs, but there was no suggestion of an echo. The atmosphere quite discomfited our man.

Norman said, "It is Major, isn't it? Or is it Doctor?"

Ramrod replied, "It's both."

No further comment passed between the two men. There was too much to be said for it to be right to speak at all. The floor upstairs was of polished cork. Ramrod had forgotten it, and it made him more nervous, which is to say more military than ever. He had done his own science, in the thirties in a very different building, in Kensington. In those days science lived in glorified gothic public lavatories with shiny tiles and vaulted corridors: an unhealthy subject, it seemed right to be housed in places that looked like isolation hospitals. The tone now seemed to be according to a new image: with a kind of subfusc simplicity, in a mansion for Mars, or the Moon.

And if it had been a mansion, then Calder's room would have counted as the bridal suite, in which there never was a bride. The photographers and silver boxes spoke eloquently of bachelorhood. Calder at fifty had the tastes of a refined undergraduate, which was something he had never been. But then he had been educated in Belfast, not at Oxford, and that is the sort of thing an ambitious academic well remembers, even when he has reached the stage of a Knighthood and an original Picasso: a stage, incidentally, which clearly seemed to Calder, this morning, in spite of the black tie and the mournful manner, only one way.

Outside the spacious carpeted office, with its huge plate glass window, they were playing cricket in the Parks. The first nets had been erected a couple of weeks before, and the tennis courts, too, had recently been marked. It pleased Calder as he pursued detailed administrative, quasi-political duties with relentless detailed quasi-political energy, that the sound of ball against bat and the raised voice of the players should come seeping into the office.

Ramrod had met him on several occasions as Sharpey had always off-loaded his official duties on to Calder's shoulders, and they talked for some time of the accident itself. It must have been half an hour later when Calder pulled down the corners of his waistcoat with the sharp tug of a man with a future, and walked over to the window. Almost with his back turned to Ramrod, who found the room rather too warm in his Curzon Street tweeds, Calder said, at last.

"You say you're making a request, Major, but my dear man, you're doing nothing of the sort. You're presenting me with Hobson's choice."

Ramrod always grew more obstinate with articulate people. He said very slowly, as if to lower the pace of their whole conversation, "I'm simply asking permission to ask questions which have to be asked."

Calder paid no attention. He was preparing his own little speech and now, with a town councillor's smug little cough, he said, "Part of our work is Classified, which means it's open to government inspection, and as you stand here as the government's representative, it would naturally be beyond my powers to prevent your coming in. But where we poor boffins may lack power these days, even in our own departments, let's hope that our advice is not considered as something to be completely ignored. I hope not . . ."

"Certainly not."

"Good. . . . Excellent. . . . Excellent," Calder muttered,

preparing himself for his next oblique salvo. "Then let me say as acting director of the labs that it cannot possibly help the work or atmosphere of the place to have a security man nosing about asking questions. I wonder if you see my point? It's simple enough. There is no hidden motive here. I am thinking only of our teachers and research men. It is my business to see that things go smoothly for them." He gave a bright, rather irrelevant smile at this point, but Ramrod replied gravely, even severely.

"Somebody paid a thousand pounds in notes to Professor Sharpey and I know the people he saw in London yesterday, and has seen in London previously. I am telling you, quite frankly, that I haven't evidence of treason. But I have indication which can't be ignored, if I'm worth my pay at all."

Ramrod smoked ten tipped cigarettes a day. He removed one carefully now from the shaped silver case which his mother had given him when he reached field rank. His family had always been more proud of the military part of his career. That a soldier could also have a scientific training had baffled them, so, like his tailor, they ignored it. He lit up.

Calder took a little time to come back with an old, old gambit: "I believe you are missing my point."

But Ramrod was sure of himself, on this ground. He asked, "Does a brief-case stuffed with fivers not arouse your curiosity?"

Calder said at once, "It doesn't surprise me, if that's what you mean," and Ramrod raised his eyebrows. He was used to more loyalty than this.

He said slowly, "Would I be right in assuming from that comment that you did not like Professor Sharpey?"

"Wrong. Absolutely wrong." Calder was enjoying himself. Paradox and surprise were part of his equipment. He liked to pose as the contradictory *enfant terrible* in all his many councils and conferences. "I liked him very much. I worked with him, off and on, for twenty years. And anybody who denies that he was one of the greatest physiologists of our times must be a fool."

He went on swiftly, throwing himself back into his swiv-
elling desk chair, "But with all his good intentions,
his pacifism, Ban the Bombism, all his leftishs, he was
as naïve politically as a child of seven. . . . And the
Americans knew how dangerous that was," he added,
waving his index finger, for emphasis. "Of course they
did. That's why they flung him out of space physiology
over there - and that was five years ago. I don't blame
them a bit."

Ramrod, however, had done all his prep. His apprecia-
tions may have been laborious, but his data was always
complete. He said, "They never proved anything against
him."

Calder rushed on. He was a better talker than listener,
unlike our man. He jumped out of his chair again as
he said, "As soon as he was back here he was meeting
all these strange gentlemen with Central European names
and snow on their boots - cultural attaches. . . . You
know the type."

But Ramrod, now as ever, fell over himself to be
fair. He wanted to inspect the labs, to ask questions
about Sharpey. But Ramrod knew the Queen's regulations
here and stuck to them. The oldest rule in the book
is that a man is innocent until he is proved guilty. Rigid
adherence to the maxim gave Ramrod a kind of austere
dignity.

He said, "Your implications are unfair, at least as
far as that period was concerned. I looked into his activities very carefully on Washington's advice. If you remember, I visited you here on more than one occasion,
ostensibly to check progress on Classified subjects, but
actually to check Sharpey. He was quite innocent then.
He had complete integrity until very recently: until
the last few months, even weeks . . ."

Ramrod now stood up. It was with a heavy sort
of sadness that he completed the description of the
old man before his death.

"Suddenly he is no longer a humane old Professor,
protesting for Peace, even if a little absurdly. He's taking
money! He's talking to the professionals from draughty

phone boxes, or on park seats." He summed it up as, "The whole chilly paraphernalia of treason," and then asked more carefully, "Isn't it reasonable that I should ask a few questions about his work here, this summer? About his closest colleagues?"

"And what makes you think they'll tell you anything?"

"I can ask."

"And disturb them. That's all you'll do. You're wasting your time asking questions. The old man was working on his own. He did not involve the others, here, whatever he was up to." Again, Ramrod gave proof of prep done.

"Doctor Longman," he said, mentioning one of the laboratory's most brilliant stars, "was with him in America, I believe?"

"He was."

"And did he work with him here?"

Calder's attitude was curious. It was possible that he was jealous of Longman. Calder was not himself an eminent research man. He said, rather huffily, "Huh! If you like to call it work!" And he laughed a little heartily. "Longman hasn't been in the lab for six weeks. I know that for a fact."

Ramrod listened, but did not comment. He asked, "Were they still working on space physiology?"

"More or less," Calder answered. "In addition to their teaching work. At least, an aspect of it. In fact they took over the building we used to call the little hut, and kept the rest of us out of it. They called it Isolation, or the Reduction of Sensation. . . ." He spoke a little haughtily. "I suppose it has some value, though I'm damned if I know quite what. We're all entitled to our views. But when you think how much down-to-earth physiology research there still remains to be done, it seems to me absurd that men as good as Sharpey should determine to put their heads a thousand miles above the clouds. . . ."

Ramrod had heard Calder on his hobby-horse before. He interrupted, but gently, " 'Isolation' could make a good starting point for me, don't you think?" He insisted, "It might throw some light on poor Sharpey.

It might even provide an answer to the question 'what is worth £1000?' . . ."

Calder, rather rudely, was glancing at some letters lying on his desk. But Ramrod wasn't easily put off.

"Longman's not in, you say?"

"I shouldn't think so, for a moment."

Ramrod paused, but Calder was still not forthcoming, so he was forced to speak again.

"Is there anybody else who might help me?"

Calder shrugged. "There's young Tate, I suppose. . . . Though it'll only take his mind off teaching, and it's been hard enough getting him on to it. Our first purpose is to teach students, you know? That's what the *brilliant* ones - the Sharpeys and the Longmans of this world - that's what they forget. They're only too keen to leave all that to poor idiots like me."

"But Tate knows the work?"

"He helped with some of the earlier low temperature stuff. Then I took him off. He's a good young teacher."

Ramrod risked a smile.

"I won't take him away for long."

"You're very insistent, Hall."

Ramrod nodded. "That's the military mind."

Calder is easily caricatured. His type, the organizer, the administrator, is never too popular. He was filled with petty ambitions. But Ramrod was made aware of the importance of his views as the pair of them came down the skeleton stairs again. The hall was filled with students passing from one demonstration to another, at the hour. They wore gowns or white coats. Their hair was untidy, their clothes eccentric and unclean. Some carried huge textbooks under their arms. They quite ignored Calder and his visitor. Their thoughts were devoted to their subject, to each other, or to Sharpey's death. Each snatch of conversation confirmed this.

When Calder asked one of them to go and tell Norman to bring the Isolation film to Lecture Theatre A, he did not obey like a recruit, like a Zombie. He nodded and asked, "Isn't Doctor Tate giving some sort of Respiration lecture in there?"

"He is," Calder said impatiently, and pointed at the modern clock above the door. "And in the five minutes in which you go to Norman and Norman returns to us, he will complete his lecture. We, also," he told the student, "can think."

The student took it very easily.

"I believe you're right," he said amazedly.

4

Tate was a good teacher, almost in spite of himself. He would have made a terrible schoolmaster. He fought his students all the time. There was no suspicion of patronage. He treated them as if they were equals in every way, and they responded to him. He called them idiots only when they were idiotic, he grew impatient with them only when there was good reason for impatience. And that was the case this morning, after the Respiration lecture in Theatre D. Most of the students had left and there were only a few crowded round the lecturer's desk, asking questions which Tate very clearly did not want them to pose. Tate himself looked tired and pouchy round the eyes. He looked more like a chronic bachelor every day.

Sun was streaming into the theatre through the big windows at the side of the room. Specks of dust rolled over in the shafts of light like stars in a whole universe subject to the same remote gravitational pull. One of the girls kept snatching at the dust in a sleepy, mid-morning way as the other students engaged Tate.

The questions, of course, concerned the Professor

on the train; why, where, and how. Tate zipped his lecture papers into his flat black brief-case in the hope of cutting the interviewers short. But one of the students was peculiarly insistent. He kept saying, "But *something* - couldn't you have done something? Couldn't you have seen it coming?"

Tate shook his head. He found Stewart, this sharp-faced boy, peculiarly trying. He was the sort of young man whose behaviour is always excessive. His manner, this morning, was, of course, excessively grave. Tate swallowed then answered, at last, "There really isn't much point in asking questions, Stewart, if the answer's obvious."

"Quite," the boy answered himself. "You couldn't see it coming. But, I mean, was he all right at Paddington?"

The girl snatching at the dust came to Tate's rescue. She simply said, "Oh, Stew —" But the boy was insistent. He missed the point, too, of her caution. Tactlessly then, he said, "Well, hell, there's no secret about all this, is there? Why shouldn't we know?"

The girl shrugged. Tate looked at her in a way any girl would have considered cold or even remote. He actually felt quite warmly towards her for trying to cut short the cross-examination. He moved his eyes back to Stewart, keeping his head quite still. It was one of his characteristics, which the students had observed and used to mimic. Tate could stand for hours absolutely stock still. At last he answered the Paddington question.

"I'd say he was tired. I noticed that."

"But d'you honestly think it was an accident?"

Tate did not reply so the boy went on, "It was after a station, wasn't it? He can't really have thought he was stepping into the corridor, not —"

Support came from an unexpected quarter, in a sharp and rasping tone. Calder had come into the lab, with Ramrod two paces to the rear. Calder said fussily, "Gentlemen, I can't approve of this sort of talk. It clearly doesn't help the lab to have this sort of gossip going on —"

Stewart was young enough to find apologies easy.

Loudly he said, "I'm sorry, sir," and started to move off. The other students went with him, asking each other who and what the gentleman like a ramrod might be. They got no clue from Calder, who waited until they had all disappeared, then took Tate by the arm, rather tightly, as if there was something a little insecure about this paternal act.

"My dear fellow," he told Tate, "you mustn't encourage that sort of talk. You shouldn't get too close to students, you know."

Tate eyed him without respect. He said, "They're naturally curious. Isn't that what we train them to be?"

"Of course, I understand," Calder replied nervously and patted Tate's shoulder. "We're all working under a sense of strain." He looked round the lab, at the blackboard, and the cinema screen which could be rolled down. He snapped his fingers and said, "We'll need that down," then suddenly asked, "You're standing in for Longman here; this should be Longman's lecture?"

Tate replied flatly, "He's ill."

Calder nodded, gave a sly little smile. "We all know Longman has his own methods," he said, "even to refusing to answer his telephone, which he did this morning. Never mind, if you've stood in for him again, you will be compensated."

Tate blinked at his senior, disapprovingly, then turned to be reintroduced to the Major.

"We have met," Ramrod said, gently, and it took a second for Tate to recognize the man who gave the orders on the cinder track. As he said "Hello" and shook hands, not very enthusiastically, Norman came swiftly into the room, with a film in his hand. He waved it vaguely at Calder, said, "I'll lace it up," and Calder then explained.

"Hall's interested in Isolation."

Ramrod smiled, even unbent a little, "If you'd care to help me a little, give me at least an outline of the work that's been done, put me in the picture?"

Tate looked him up and down, and thought what an absurd, stuffed-looking duck he was. "I certainly

can't lecture on it. I don't know much more than you,
I'm sure."

Ramrod said, "I know nothing."

"That's what I meant."

Tate's solid unhelpfulness made Calder interrupt once
more.

"It's only a question of showing the film, Tate; perhaps
elucidating any point the Major wants to ask about."

Tate frowned. "Sharpey's film?" he asked. It somehow
seemed wrong to show Sharpey on film, this morning.
Norman answered from the projector. "I hope so, because
it's laced up. The first Isolation job he did. Ready when
you are."

Tate raised his eyebrows. "Then we'd better pull
down the blinds."

As he moved across to the big windows, Calder
left, asking Hall to return to his room, afterwards, so
they could go to college together, for some lunch. Ramrod
thanked him, then strolled across to the windows, ostensibly to help Tate with the blind.

He said, "I gather Doctor Longman worked with
Sharpey, in the States."

Tate said, "That blind comes down a little farther
if you pull."

The 16-mm film, introducing Ramrod to Isolation
must also have been one of the lab's first ventures with
celluloid. It was an amateurish piece of work. The
lighting was erratic, and the sound, too, was blaring
at one moment then vague and muffled at the next. But
Ramrod learnt a lot.

It opened with an arctic scene that frankly might
have come from any film library, marked "snow", "arctic", or "antarctic". There was wind and snow, and
low light. Through this struggled three or four men and
a sledge drawn by those inevitable arctic dogs that
bark, and get told "Moosh!" The figures were unrecognizable as they staggered to a curious little hut, made of
boxes, planks, and corrugated iron, half buried in the
drifts. There the party stopped, and disappeared into

the darkness of this house. When they reappeared they brought with them a stiff, dazed, corpselike figure, and covering him with blankets, propped him on the sledge. It was impossible to tell whether the man was dead or alive. The commentary, meantime, explained.

"The arctic circle in April 1960. This is the hut where an extremely brave French geo-physicist, Doctor Jean Bonvoubois, spent the winter of 1959-60. He spent the last four months of it alone, in almost perpetual darkness. A small party of us relieved Doctor Bonvoubois that spring."

With his eyes still on the screen Ramrod asked, "Could that be Sharpey commentating?"

"That could be."

There was a close-up then of Bonvoubois; an effigy, a drawn ghost of a man. Then the sledge moved off.

The scene switched sharply to the cabin of a ship, obviously the party's base ship, because here, self-consciously, in front of the camera, Professor Sharpey was settling Bonvoubois in a chair behind a long table. Bonvoubois was conscious. Whether he was properly alive was less certain, as the film then showed. He was a frail looking man with curiously telling eyes. He had long thin white fingers which he laid on the table as if they were not part of him, but a prop he had brought along. Tate then joined the party, sitting awkwardly on the table in order to get into the scene. He held a notebook and pencil, and also looked anxiously at the camera, for a moment; exactly like somebody in a home movie. A steward then flashed on and off the screen, putting some cocoa in front of Bonvoubois, who seemed to have no idea what it was or why it was there. Sharpey was considerably more robust at this time, almost cocky. The moustache which looked so sad towards the end of his life was less noticeable because he was wearing a beard as well. How Tate ever managed to shave in that climate remained a mystery to all, although his students, when they saw the film, suggested that he was not old enough to shave anyway. He certainly looked younger than half of them. But it was Bonvoubois, on the screen, who drew the attention. He seemed peculiarly ill co-ordinated, almost paralysed, and dreadfully unhappy. He wagged his head from side to side, occasionally with a little, animal moan. Sharpey, in his commentary, continued to explain:

"At that time, our party was interested in the effects of low temperature. We simply wanted to know what happens to people and animals when the thermometer drops far below zero. The applications of such knowledge could be useful in anything from modern surgery to space travel. Doctor Tate and I interviewed Bonvoubois a few hours after we had found him in his hut. This film was taken at the time. Please notice his behaviour."

As the camera jumped and jerked and drew a little closer, Bonvoubois kept his eyes downcast. He was quite ageless; as frail as a child, as abstracted as a saint. With a thump, the camera came to rest and Bonvoubois looked up, his eyes light and hostile. Sharpey put a hand on his shoulder to give him confidence. He looked up at him as if he had never seen him before and completely distrusted him. Behind, there were noises of the ship creaking, and the sound track, taken at the time, was very hard to decipher.

Sharpey said something like, "Look here, don't pay any attention to the camera. Try and relax," and Tate offered the poor man some of the cocoa. In fact he more than offered, he definitely ordered him to take a drink of it, and after a pause, Bonvoubois, childlike, obeyed. Sharpey seemed to be greatly disturbed by the man's condition and started to comfort him again, but Tate interrupted to ask the scientist's questions.

"Where do you think you are?"

Bonvoubois seemed to be trying to understand. He frowned, moaned, rocked from side to side. It was not as if he were crying then, but merely, painfully thawing out. Tears began to pour down his face and Sharpey, obviously, at this moment was considering cancelling the filming. He looked nervously at Tate, then at the camera, saying tentatively, "It may be too soon."

Tate shook his head. "He'll be all right," he said.

"It's important to get something down." Those were the days when Tate was a research man, not a teacher. He watched himself now, impassively, but the character on the screen was slightly different: a more purposeful person altogether.

On the screen, Tate started to question Bonvoubois again.

"Tell us your name. D'you know what you're called?"

"Yes," Bonvoubois replied, at last. "What? . . . Yes, I . . ."

"Tell us your name, please. Full name. Monsieur, comment vous appelez vous?"

Bonvoubois looked very vague and remote. But then suddenly he brightened up. Perkily, almost like a spinster at a tea party, he said, "I speak English very well."

Tate followed the experiment relentlessly.

"Good. Then perhaps you'd tell us your name."

Bonvoubois nodded, smiled, and waited. Then as Sharpey was about to interrupt again, the answer came clearly and suddenly.

"My name is Doctor Jean Bonvoubois. . . . Yes. . . . What am I drinking? What is this?"

Sharpey said, "Cocoa," gently, but Tate was a little impatient with the old man's soft methods. They obviously did no good, but merely allowed the Frenchman to slip back into limbo-land.

"D'you know how long you were in the hut?"

"Cocoa . . ." was all Bonvoubois answered, staring at the cup.

"How many days?"

Again Sharpey intervened, "One moment, please, Tate, we are not here to bully a man into answering our questions, even if we think them important. But, Monsieur Bonvoubois, you should try to think back and help us. I'm sorry we have to bother you —"

"Tant pis . . . You're right . . ." He laughed. He seemed sleepy, now. "The scientists asked the question because the scientists wanted to know . . ."

"We want to know how long you think you were alone in that hut," Sharpey said, and again Bonvoubois

suddenly came to life, as if somewhere within him a
huge dynamo had begun to turn over. He leant forward
over the table and said with great fervour, "Alone? . . .
I am not alone. Jamais! A few days to begin with,
maybe. Seven, ten, I don't remember well. But after
that I am not alone, no, no, no. Because he come."

Tate and Sharpey exchanged a glance. They knew
very well that nobody could have visited the scientist
during the winter.

Tate asked him "Who? Who came?" But after his
fervent outburst, he seemed to have slipped away again.
His eyelids fluttered. Tate had to shake his arm and
his long fingers fell on the table like a puppet's legs,
almost with a rattle.

"Who?"

He groaned. "He came. When things were bad. He
came. We'd talk. We'd sing. The old songs."

"Who was he? This man that visited you?"

"No man. An angel."

Again the two examiners exchanged glances. The
reply interested them, and Tate leant back and made
a note. He was of course entirely sceptical of the religious
significance and Bonvoubois read this on his face. He
pointed at Tate. "He doesn't know," he said. "Look
at his face. He knows nothing. Nothing." He paused
as if he was gathering energy to say something else,
then suddenly closed his eyes. Tate touched the cold,
fine white hands, but there was no reaction; nothing more
than a little groan.

"He's asleep."

Suddenly there was a blank, a flash, then continued
flashing, at the end of the first reel, and in the theatre,
Ramrod asked if he might be permitted to smoke.

"Of course," Tate said, and then turned back to
the screen as the film continued.

Professor Sharpey was standing outside the Biology
lab on a windy afternoon. His grey hair was blowing
about, but otherwise he looked very spruce in a bow
tie and clean white coat. He was holding a microphone,
addressing the camera directly.

"He had gone to the Arctic Circle to investigate the hazards of life at eighty below zero." He smiled the cheerful smile of the enterprising almost nineteenth-century-type scientist. "And we bungled it! We don't look back to those next months with pride. It is very easy to get too close to a subject. We set up some experiments."

The scene now switched to one of the laboratories, upstairs, in which these experiments were carried out, and Sharpey's voice continued as a commentary. A student lay on a slab in a huge refrigerator looking very much like the pictures we see of astronauts in training with wire attachments to their pulse, heart, and head. Outside this fridge, Tate and Sharpey stood checking the controls and preparing a second student for his ordeal. Sharpey's voice continued, "Our object was to simulate the conditions under which Bonvoubois had lived in the Arctic. We set up an almost totally dark cubicle, which was in fact a refrigerator. For different periods and at different temperatures we observed the effects on our subjects - measuring all those things you might expect; body temperature, blood pressure, pulse rate. We used ordinary students who volunteered to undergo the tests. To a more or less marked degree, each showed similar symptoms of disorientation and confusion of the mind to Bonvoubois."

Again the scene switched to show Tate examining a student before he was subjected to a spell in the refrigerator, and after it. The student was asked the same simple questions, but in the second interview he failed to answer correctly what seven times four should make.

Again Sharpey appeared on screen, addressing the camera, standing in front of the refrigerator. He said, with a smile, "It was at this point that Doctor Harry Longman, whose research at this time was devoted to high altitude physiology, walked through our lab. He asked a very simple question."

The effect was slightly spoilt by the amateur technicians who must have been too ambitious here. As Sharpey stood back the sound boom came swinging across the screen and just caught the Professor's head. Stepping forward in front of the camera, Longman ducked, looked at the boss, then in a pleasant, deep American voice remembered his line.

"What makes you think it's got anything to do with temperature?" he asked, with a charming smile. He was a big lean man, with dark eyes and hair that had some grey in it. He looked very relaxed and happy. Ramrod, at the edge of his seat, regarded him with special interest. But now Sharpey was in close-up again.

"It hadn't anything to do with low temperature," he said, raising his eyebrows at his own stupidity. "Bonvoubois and our student guinea pigs had been affected not by the cold but by their prolonged isolation. One week later we changed the name of the laboratory outside our main building to 'Isolation'."

There was a shot then of the main building and the curious single-storied prefabricated building outside in which, later, were to take place some of the most frightening scientific experiments ever carried out in this country. It was clear to Ramrod and Tate, watching the film that morning, that Sharpey had not then any idea of the sort of tragedies this work would involve. He looked serious, but not grave, a picture of an Oxford professor in a tweed suit as he came forward to the camera to finish the training film.

"By 'Isolation' we mean the study of what happens to a man when you deprive him of all sensations. We want to know what happens to him if he sees nothing, feels nothing, tastes nothing, hears nothing, and smells nothing. We want to know what happens to the body and particularly to the Central Nervous System when a man is put into complete isolation, with the sort of conditions that may well be experienced, for instance, in space flight. To do this we invented a perfectly simple piece of apparatus —"

Simple, perhaps, but eerie and dreadful too. The scene switched to the torture chamber; more precisely to Isolation, Lab A. One of the windows was open but the light reflecting against the huge central tank made the whole place look more weird. The shutters on the windows were thick, the walls were sound-proofed. It was a place for political police, not for scientists. There were streaks of dust on some of the felting round the doors, there were three chairs and a trestle table that could have come from any barracks. But these were dwarfed by the big aluminium tank in the middle of the room.

Sharpey simply said, "When a man is submerged in this tank all sensations can be reduced to a minimum. He is utterly isolated; lonely, bewildered. Studying his behaviour under these conditions we find we have stepped into a new and frightening world."

The camera picked out then, the rubber suit and mask, like a frogman's which the subject used to wear. There were ropes above, hanging down into the tank. Sharpey said, "We seem to be dealing with the physics of the soul."

The film faded, there was another flash, then in lettering, END OF ISOLATION, PART I. Again there was a small technical hitch of the old home-movie kind. Numbers flashed across the white screen, 9, 8, 7, 6, 5, 4, 3, 2, 1, END.

Ramrod was sitting quite still in his place when the projector had been switched off and whirred to a standstill. Tate pulled up the blind and the spring sun came blazing in.

Ramrod asked, at last, "Is there more film?"

"No."

And Norman, the lab boy, spoke, from behind the projector. "Sharpey hoped to do one this summer, but he couldn't have, anyway."

"Why not?"

"The experiments are still incomplete."

"You worked in Isolation?"

"I'm part of the equipment," the lab boy said.

"I forget your name."

Norman answered as if seriously, "Roger Casement," but Ramrod did not think it was a time for humour. Colouring a little, he turned back to Tate.

"Did you continue to work on isolation after the first stages?"

"For a while. The old man, Longman, and me."

"No students?"

"Just the three of us, and Norman, here. At first it seemed rather fun."

"And at the end? Not such fun?"

Tate should have been a lawyer.

"At the end only Longman and Sharpey were on it."

"Then only Sharpey?"

Tate shrugged. "I've no doubt Calder's told you that it's some weeks since Longman's been in."

"How many weeks?"

Tate looked up at Norman who said, "Don't look at me, son. The lab boy doesn't check the professor in and out."

"About how long?"

Tate said, "About six weeks."

Ramrod climbed to his feet a little stiffly. "You've been very helpful," he said, formally, then he went on, "I think it would be useful if I could have a word with Longman. Would you please ask him to call me? Calder knows where to find me. . . ."

Tate nodded, but not very graciously.

"I'd be grateful," Ramrod said, as he went out.

At the back of the room Norman had the film in the can. He was looking round a cupboard filled with equipment, films, and tapes for the different lectures.

Tate said wearily, "I'm always used as the fag round here."

Norman came pacing down the shallow steps, then stepped beside his senior, delighted by the situation, pleased to use him as his servant. He had some tape recordings in his hand.

He said, "And while you're going, doctor, you might give Mrs. Longman these tapes."

Tate took them, "What are they?"

Norman said, "Sir Malcolm Sargent at Helsinki, pinched without permission from the BBC. One of the bi-products of our excellent recorders in Isolation: no echo, no faults. She's been shouting for them for months but I never get time to get up to their place . . . Cheer up, doctor."

Tate frowned. "I've got work to do. I've got Collections to mark. I've —"

"Doctor," Norman said with a sly smile, "if you think that I think that you don't want to see Oonagh Longman again, then, doctor, you're wrong."

Tate was stung. He blushed like a boy.

At 1445 hours after an inadequate and indigestible meal in Calder's college common room, Ramrod withdrew - for a Major never retreats - to his cold hotel room, sat on the hard high bed and firmly *Reappreciated*. He swallowed a glass of bisodol, an old soldier's best friend, and tried to bring his thoughts to bear. There were so many new factors that he could not yet discipline them under their correct headings. He therefore tried a disorganized informal run-through. He did better than any of the young scientists would have expected. But then it is always easy to underestimate old soldiers. The ex-general pottering about his conservatory with a portable typewriter makes more money out of his writing than all the thousand brilliant young playwrights and novelists stuffed into Nottingham attics.

The film puzzled more than impressed him, which was not perhaps too surprising, as the only thing that really impressed him were pantomimes on ice and actors flying in Peter Pan. "Damn clever," he'd say of them, or sometimes, "Damnably clever."

He had, of course, known more about isolation than he liked to pretend, and he had felt the weirdness of that tank room. Who wouldn't have, watching the film on the morning following Sharpey's death? But his mind stuck at one sentence which did not convince him. It was Sharpey's only example of the possible applications of this work. "Similar," he had said, or something of the sort. "Similar to the sort of conditions which a man might experience in space flight." Now Ramrod knew the Queen's enemies with whom he was dealing - the ones that had lunched Sharpey so frequently in London - and one thing he was sure about was that these enemies would hardly be needing information about space flights, not from the English. On the other hand, he found it difficult to see what the applications of isolation might be if space flight were ruled out. What, in other words, had been worth one thousand pounds in notes, unless it was the old man himself? And what had Sharpey told them that he should be so filled with remorse as to throw himself out of the train?

A re-examination of what isolation exactly meant gave Ramrod a clue, at least. In fact the tank simply acted as a kind of super-dark cell, in which a prisoner might be put in solitary confinement. When the man came out he was disorientated and in extreme cases seemed to suffer from hallucinations. The applications of this did not sound so startling. It might be a quick method of extracting the truth from somebody, but granted that there were also hallucinations, it could be rather a risky method. Ramrod knew other, older ways. He had used them, too, even if, like the best policemen, he preferred to forget them.

He paced up and down the little bedroom, the floor of which was at a ridiculous angle, running away from the windows. He tried a penny and it rolled all the way down to the bed post. This relaxation seemed to give him courage to conclude: not space flight country, not that, at all. The thousand pounds had been paid for something to do with bending minds. He put the tooth mug and bisodol on to the basin shelf and with a belch that shook the walls, bravely left the room to return to the labs and Sharpey's documents.

5

There was once a rather famous Oxford couple who lived up the Banbury Road during the war, and they could only make love to the strains of Sibelius First, which, musically, builds - to say the least of it. One day their two-year-old son, perhaps even more precocious than most don's children, dug his heels through the records. As if searching for blood for a transfusion the couple went round all the shops in Oxford, then in London, but at that time, of course, there were few recordings being made. At last, after a dreadful expedition up the Portobello Road, they knew they would have to try without music, and did so, after changing at Didcot into that slow train without corridors where so many undergraduates take a violent leap into adulthood. But without music, passion escaped them, and a few months later, the marriage, understandably, came to an end.

Tate often considered erotic conundrums of this sort as he bicycled about Oxford, accusing himself of a dullness and lack of emotional adventure which could almost count as arrested development. He observed himself closely, if not quite closely enough. He knew that he would be returning to the arctic at the end of term, and that was no climate for love. And although he always considered himself in this ironic, unfavourable way - Jack, he is a dull, dull boy - he knew only too well that there was something more seriously unrestful inside him, which sooner or later was going to come out. He hoped he would not live a bachelor don until his late fifties, then make grabs at students of both sexes. This was not infrequent in the academic circles in which he spent his life, but he considered it vulgar, if not depraved. He also knew that this disturbance inside, this odd, undefined urge to do something ludicrous, even humiliating, had only existed for a year or eighteen months. He had considered change of temperature arctic to Oxford, as a source. But more likely, he thought, it had to do with his new work. That he was the best teacher in the lab was, he knew, a condemnation. He had been helpful enough both in Low Temperature and Isolation, but Sharpey and Longman as research men, were in a different class altogether. His future, once he had admitted this to himself, was a dull, even a crotchety one.

He would remain a fellow of his college, continue keeping up with new physiological advances, and read fundamentally the same lectures to science and medical students until his hair grew grey and dry, and his tweed jacket gave way at the seams. It was a fair enough life, he supposed. He shouldn't complain. But it is not easy to keep a sanguine temperament in such a limited field when next door, new young men would be reaching towards Nobel prizes. He felt lonely at the prospect of the life he had chosen for himself before he had recognized his own intellectual limitation. Calder, once, must have done the same.

What he did not notice about himself was that these thoughts were always strongest when he cycled up Walton Street, beyond the Scala cinema. The Longmans' house was there, beyond Tackley Place. He also did not recognize that the dissatisfaction he felt, comparing his own lot to Longman's, was not singly or even mainly on account of the other's professional reputation.

Tate dismounted at the gate of their terrible North Oxford house, built with the rest of them up there in the early part of the century when Keble College's lavatory bricks were still the rage. He took the tape from his basket and put his cycle clips in his pocket which already held all sorts of boyish things, like a penknife, a roll of copper wire, and a couple of boiled sweets. Then he paused for a moment, outside the gate, to inspect a huge maroon coloured veteran, if not vintage, Lagonda car, which was new to him. It must have dated back to the end of the twenties sometime, but it was polished, like new. Then his attention was attracted by the noise that was part of the Longman household, and which he remembered with pleasure, even with a little lift of his heart. Before he got his barge, where he now lived, Tate had lodged with the Longmans and he knew their children very well. They were all healthily undernourished, with unending energy and sticks for limbs, each outgrowing his or her clothes which would be handed down to the next, regardless of sex.

This afternoon they were playing on the lawn which looked like a weedy meadow. They had fitted up a sail on a raft-like structure, but it was only when Tate approached them more closely and read the name of the raft, that he fully understood. In bold if unequal letters, it read K O N T I K I. The children's names all began with P, and three Longmans were there, with several other neighbours who looked much the same as all Oxford children in the spring - pale faced, long haired, with blazing eyes.

They soon spotted him, but they did not give him a warm welcome. They were too committed to the raft and Pacific journey to do that. They nodded thoughtfully when he said "Hello," so he raised his eyebrows and called them a jolly unfriendly lot. He hadn't seen them for nearly two months.

"Is your father in?"

Penny, one of the middle ones, aged eight, then turned to her younger brother and asked, "Port beam, Thor, what is it?"

Paul raised an old and huge telescope which most likely was the first source of the whole complicated fantasy.

"Nothing," he said. "Just another bloody baracenda."

Persephone, the oldest, was consulting the text. As Tate turned away from them she was saying, "In a very few pages, now, we have the second storm. Somebody

ought to take a few reefs in the canvas." There followed
much activity with the old cotton sheet which had a
hole scorched in the middle of it. In the distance, carried
by the breeze, was a faint sound of applause. Somebody,
either a schoolboy or an undergraduate, must have
scored a boundary, or been bowled out. It should have
been ten past three, but in fact it was almost an hour
later than that.

As Tate entered the house he rang, but the bell
did not work so he walked some paces into the hall,
calling out, "Is anybody at home?" Then he stopped,
amazed by what he saw. Peers, the youngest child, was
thoughtful but perfectly contented looking. He was pedalling round and round the hall on his tricycle. He
paid no attention to Tate, but there was nothing unusual
about this. Peers never said much to anybody and tri-
cycling in circles was his pleasure. The amazing thing
was the state of the house. There was no carpet on
the floor, but a campbed and some toys round it. There
was a sleeping bag and some cushions nearby. Tate
frowned and peeped into the first room, which used
to be the dining-room. Here, too, there was an air of
pandemonium. It was as if upstairs had become an
untidy downstairs; as if the children had captured the
lower floor and driven the grown-ups elsewhere. A
moment later, when he called again, Tate gathered that
the adults must be seeking refuge upstairs. There was
a movement, an opening of a door and through the
bannister running along the landing he saw a pair of
bare feet approaching. They were bare feet and the
bare legs above them were only then, at the last moment,
covered with a towel dressing gown. The sight of them
made Tate squeeze the tips of his fingers into his palms,
he did not know why. Oonagh Longman was standing
at the top of the stairs pulling the dressing gown cord
tightly round her waist when he recovered himself enough
to look up again. She had asked, "Who is it?" as she
approached. Now pushing back her long thick brown
hair she answered herself, "Oh, it's you."

"Tate," Tate said - good dull boy - "Tate in time

for tea." He sounded quite nervous, as if he had come
to court her.

She said, "You'd better come upstairs."

"Not a very warm welcome after so long," he said,
as he obeyed.

She turned away, casually, as she answered, "No?
I'm sorry. It wasn't meant that way."

She led him to a room which he knew well. It
was the spare bedroom in which he had once stayed,
in the days before the children had commandeered the
ground floor. He noticed that a sofa and a couple of
armchairs had been hauled upstairs, although the bed
was still in the room. It had been shoved into the darkest
corner where the ceiling followed the slope of the roof.
She switched on the electric fire, pulled back the curtains,
and sniffed and blinked as if she were surprised by
daylight. She stood listening to the noise from the cricket
match far away, then turned back into the room, saying,
"I'd give you a cigarette but we smoked them all last
night."

He said, "You?"

"Didn't I used to smoke?"

"Never."

She smiled vaguely and decided to sit down on the
white rug by the fire. "Things have changed," she said.
As he looked down at her, he caught sight for a moment
of her breasts. They were warm and smooth and made
to look browner by the white towelling of the dressing
gown, which she now pulled more tightly around her.
Tate knew - very well, he knew - that this was her first
appearance that day, but this knowledge was not only
imparted by her nakedness. It was the warmth of her,
the aroma, if not exactly the smell that confirmed it
for him, and he felt for a second desperately jealous
of all other people's passions and the calm pitch of
their subsequent happiness. Determined, however, to
disguise this, he moved over to the window, refusing
to let himself stare at her face and long hair, or imagine
the round, soft nakedness below.

She was thirty now, and originally came from Orkney

or Shetland or Finland, or one of those places where
the wind blows a girl until she has the look of a modern
statue. The face was moulded so that it had the least
possible wind resistance. She was like a pretty girl
caught in a wind tunnel. Her cheeks swept away like
wings, her hair was pulled straight back from her forehead
as she fixed it now in a loose bun at the nape of her
neck. Her eyes were rather elongated and when she
smiled they almost disappeared. But they were very
bright and grey or green, depending on the surrounding
light. In the Arctic or wherever it was she lived, no
doubt they would look green. She had a small nose
and fairly full soft lips. There were a few freckles,
now, in May and by August there would be more. Her
body was a little too generous to be either fashionable
or resistible and her legs were almost chunky, but they
had a strength and simplicity which Tate had not forgotten.
She had a pet name which Longman, and sometimes
the children, called her and it was never more apt than
this afternoon: Otter.

Tate was anxious to know if she had heard of Sharpey's
death, but he stopped himself asking her directly because
he suspected his own motives. He knew he wanted somehow
to destroy that very certain happiness which no one
could have failed to recognize. In fact, he already knew
that she could not know about Sharpey. He skirted the
subject, speaking in very matter of fact tones.

"I think Calder's been trying to get hold of Longman."

She was like an actress slow on her cues. Her voice
seemed to come a long, long way, and her answers arrived
a beat late.

"We took the receiver off some time last week. We're
deeply uncommitted to the world just now." Then
she looked towards the window, listening to the sound
of more applause.

"What's that noise?"

For a second Tate hesitated, again about to burst
the bubble with the news. Then he put the Sibelius
tape down on the window sill and seemed to resign

himself to answering her. "Cricket." He wanted to say more, but stuck there.

"How depressing," she answered, and shifted on the rug, tucking a leg beneath her. "I think I'll try and persuade Longman we should go to Mexico."

It sounded unlikely, but dons know dons' wives' pipe-dreams. Tate relaxed a little for the first time to ask, "Is he persuadable at present?" And then he wished he had not said it. He had given her the cue to say all the things her body already said: all the things he did not want to hear. She talked with much more vigour, almost with a glow.

"He's never been so persuadable," she said, and from a side table she had grabbed the end of a bar of chocolate. She ate it and crumpled the paper on her lap, resting her hands flat on it as she prepared to tell him more. It was a gesture of rare, almost inexpressible joy. "Do you know we've spent every single day and night together for forty-seven days?"

Tate looked away again. He said very softly, "I imagine that occasionally happens with married couples."

Oonagh did not seem to hear the note of discouragement. She tipped back her head and said, "I think I am glad you called. I think it is very nice to see you. It's an extra pleasure telling somebody about it. I hadn't thought of that. . . . We haven't been apart that whole forty-seven days. D'you know we've bought a beautiful old car? A Lagonda. Doesn't it sound like a goddess? And did you know Longman's a marvellous driver? We sometimes take the children and shout at people and - not in the evening, though. Not at night. We go alone, then. Last night the headlights got quite covered with midges and things. . . ."

"Oonagh —"

She looked up at him, less than friendly, suddenly. Tate spoke again.

"Tell me what's going on."

She shook her head and smiled wearily. "It's silly to try and ask you to understand. You of all people."

"I thought I was a friend."

She did not answer that, but instead, asked him inconsequentially, "How old are you, Tate?"

"Nearly as old as you."

"No, you're not old at all," she replied. "You're like poor dear old Sharpey. Suspended between man and boy, forever - pure scientist."

The mention of the name could have given Tate his cue, but he was afraid, somehow, to take it. He felt the distressing news would somehow be laid on his back. She would hate him for it, nobody else, and in her presence he could not entertain the thought of that. She spoke again.

"I am in love, Tate. Does that mean anything to you?"

She had to answer for him. "No. Nothing. Like pain, it's incommunicable. I am in love." There were no blushes; there was no shyness as she went on, "I never knew what the world was like until now. Really I didn't. Maybe when I was seventeen. No, not even then. I wasn't aware of it like this. Even food tastes different. You can't understand, of course, you can't. Let's not exhaust ourselves talking about it."

And suddenly now, she did look exhausted. Tate sat down for the first time. He said, "You've certainly had some sort of experience, or else you've gone weak in the head. This I grant you. The evidence stares me in the face. What I used to know as a perfectly normal house has been turned - but almost literally - turned upside down. The sitting rooms are upstairs and the bedrooms and nurseries seem to be downstairs. You're rising at half past four in the afternoon. I'm sorry if I appear to be dim but I still can't quite fathom the cause of all this."

She looked at him oddly, as if he were perhaps a deaf man, but she did not say "I am in love" again. Instead she got to her feet, and smiled.

"Not to worry about it, poor old Tatty. I'm going to make coffee. Longman's next door. You'd better go and dig him out."

"Longman?" Tate said, standing up again. "You used to call him things ruder than that."

Almost sharply she replied, "Oh, but I've lost my sense of humour. That's part of it."

6

Tate expected the bedroom to be in disorder, but it was worse than that. It was in open mutiny. Shirts, shoes, underclothes, trousers, and dresses were parked or hung over tables, chair, and bed - a big, big, unmade bed. Longman himself was sitting in pyjamas and woolly dressing gown on a small balcony outside. Expecting Oonagh, he called back "Darling?" without turning round, and Tate said, "It isn't her," as he came out to the verandah which was altogether too small for Longman. His big feet were resting on the balustrade and he sat with the deck chair tipped back on two legs. His hair, which was long for an American's, brushed the brick-work behind. He had only the trace of an accent.

Below, the children had left the *Kon Tiki* to play hide-and-seek in some pacific isle. Their voices came and went, and the applause from the cricket field occasionally drifted across. There were some pine trees at this side of the house, forming a tall dark screen, and the midges were already dancing round in their curious, separate constellations. Longman clapped his hands to drive some away.

"Damned midges," he said. "Always make me cry." But he did not look the sort of man who would cry very easily. He had a big lean face with a long jaw.

His eyes were brown, slightly humorous, even lazy in their movements. He did not shift his feet from the ugly wooden balustrade, but tied a new knot with his dressing gown cord and asked, "What brings you?"

Tate had brought through the tapes. He said, "Malcolm Sargent at Helsinki, in the first place; fagging for Norman."

"Oh, yes." Longman did not believe a word of it. He looked steadily at his friend with a kind of benevolent suspicion. "That's very kind. Dump 'em on *The Times* there."

The papers had not been opened. Tate picked them up, saying, "You haven't read them?"

"No."

Again Tate did not seem to have the courage to pass bad news. He did not know what a rare restraint this was; most people are delighted to tell their friends the worst. But Tate knew how badly Longman would feel it. Whatever drove Sharpey, one thing was certain, that at the end he was working far too hard. Norman had mentioned it on several occasions, but somehow nobody had done anything about it. Longman, after all, was the one who should have done something. He was meant to be on Isolation, too.

Again Longman gave Tate a long searching look, and he guessed there might be something in the papers. But he spoke as idly as before. "It's amazing how out of touch one can get, in North Oxford, if one tries."

"I can imagine."

Longman refused to fish for information. It was as if he had reached the brink of reality after a long, long convalescence and did not quite dare cross it. In his eyes there was something approaching fear, now. The children's voices drifted up. One of them was counting backwards, allowing the others to hide. Bad news, dread, even disaster seemed to hang with the midges in that heavy air.

"We've got a new car," Longman said. "New in 1928."

"We've got a new man interested in Isolation, one

Major Hall, a Curzon Street bloodhound, which means Mi squared." Tate leant on the balustrade and looked down on the children scurrying about the jungle that had once been a garden. Penny's voice floated up. She counted forwards now. "Fifty-seven, fifty-eight, fifty-nine - Coming!"

Tate said, "He's also interested in this Sharpey affair." He continued to look over the balcony. Longman at last lowered his feet.

"What about Sharpey?"

Penny's voice came up again as she started her search "Com-ing - com-ing." Then she stopped underneath the balcony and shouted up to Tate. "Tatty, I'll give you a penny if you tell me. Can you see them from there?"

Tate said, "Threepence."

"Tuppence."

"All right."

"Where?" she said.

"Nowhere," he said. "I can't see one of them, honestly."

"Oh, that's cheating."

"You still owe me tuppence," he shouted, but she ran off in a huff.

Longman said, "Answer, Tate."

Tate turned and handed him the folded newspaper. He said, "The answer's in there."

"Not good news?"

Tate said, a little edgily, "It's *real* news." Then he moved into the bedroom.

"I'll go and help Oonagh with the coffee. I gather it's breakfast time."

The kitchen was the one good room in the house. It had been modernized when the Longmans moved in, and it had big sunny windows. There was even a dish washer, a rare luxury in North Oxford. Oonagh was putting huge cups on to a tray when Tate came down.

She said, "I know from your face you've told him something horrible."

"If I have, must I be blamed for it?"

She seemed to answer "yes" by refusing to answer at all. He went on. "I think it's a bit rough that the first messenger from real life should get it in the neck."

She said, "Somebody brought news of a father's death to a son, expecting a reward, and got his head chopped off. Was that English history, or Scandinavian myth? I went to altogether too many schools. . . ." Then looking at him hard she added, "If you've upset him now, Tate, truly, I'll never forgive you. I won't be able to."

"Why 'now'? There's something you haven't told me. There's the most peculiar atmosphere —"

"There's nothing wrong," she said. "I told you. He's happy."

Tate did not quite dare say that Longman looked far from happy to him but she read it from his face and insisted again, "He is. I'm serious. I'm not lying. You say you're a messenger from reality, but it's real enough - maybe every woman dreams of an affair like this after twelve years."

"An affair?"

"That's what it is. Unless you know another word to describe the situation."

But Tate did not wish to hear it described any more. He interrupted, to say, "Frankly, I didn't bring very good news."

"What?"

"If you opened your newspapers, you'd know. I left him with it."

"Tell me."

Tate shook his head. "He'd better do that, honestly."

She seemed to accept that easily. She wanted any news and all news to be told her by Longman, by nobody else. She was surprisingly competent in the kitchen. She unplugged the percolator, and put the hot milk in a jug. Tate stood about, restless and unhappy. She talked to him as if he were a child, not a man staring and staring at her.

"Coffee. . . . Wake up. Be a good boy and carry up the tray." As he took it, she smiled and said, "I don't know how people believe you're a don. You look more like a serious schoolboy every day."

When they came through, Longman was in the hall. He was still in his dressing gown, but he had pulled trousers and jacket on, over his pyjamas.

Tate stopped, at once, to see how the other had taken the news and Oonagh paused, too. They found themselves suspended for a moment longer at the edge of the cliff, watching Peers tricycle round and round.

Longman was sitting on the stairs, talking to his son in a dreamy sort of way, saying, "You'll get giddier and giddier." They were like deaf people at a noisy fair, staring blankly at each other; all except Peers, who kept on pedalling.

"Round and round," his father said. "I don't know how you do it, or why. You'll get so giddy, my friend, that you'll be sitting on the ceiling."

Peers gave a slow smile. He appeared to enjoy that idea very much, and cycling still he lowered his chin on to the handlebars and stared up at the ceiling. Oonagh broke this curious pause. She said "Coffee," and grabbed the tray as if she could bear it no longer, but she went too quickly and on the second step she tripped and fell and the cups and percolator crashed down to the ground. She yelled a word which Tate would not have guessed that she had ever known, and the following explosion made even Peers stay still. Oonagh was ridiculously upset. Some of the coffee had spilt down her white dressing gown. Longman held her by the shoulders and said, "It doesn't matter, it doesn't matter," but she kept her head down, saying, "It does," as she picked up the pieces of her favourite cups. Tate, alarmed by the nervous pitch of her reaction, went back to the kitchen to get a cloth, and Peers was glad to come with him.

Oonagh was a superstitious person. Her fears were too deeply ingrained for Longman ever to exorcize them altogether, and though she could not name any particular superstition - no mirror, for example, had been broken - she seemed to feel afraid, and shaken. Then very suddenly and rationally, when Tate had returned and they were all wiping the stained carpet with a wet cloth, she said:

"I know there's something worse coming. I'd better have that straight away."

Longman stared at her. There was an extraordinary telepathy between the two. Often they astonished their friends, quite unconsciously, but Tate had never witnessed a more stunning example than this. Longman never opened his mouth. Then after the pause she said, "Death? . . . Sharpey?" and began to scrub a little harder. A moment later Longman took her upstairs, by the hand, to show her *The Times'* report. Tate, meantime, went back to the kitchen to make more coffee, on Longman's instructions. Peers was still cycling round, in there.

Oonagh took a long time reading the report. It was as if she had to read it several times to understand it, then at last she reacted as if the words had been quite meaningless.

She said, "I didn't know he got the Nobel."

"Years ago."

She said, almost excitedly, "You know, I've always meant to confess this. I think half the reason I married you was because I thought you were going to be a great scientist."

He stared at her tenderly. He knew all these feminine covering tricks. He helped her now to speak about nothing. There were too many questions to be asked about Sharpey and about what his death might mean.

Jokingly about great scientists, he said, "Give the boy time."

Quite unsmilingly she replied, "I used to meet the other girls and they'd say about this fellow or that hat. . . . They'd gossip. I'd be talking about this fellowship or that research. I listened to you that much. I married science that much. They should have had articles in women's journals about me. I really took an interest in your work."

"Well, go on —"

"Was I going to say something?"

"You seemed to be warming up."

She said, "I don't care a damn for your science, any more. Not half a damn. I'd really rather you were a waiter. Are you going to the labs tomorrow?"

"I don't know yet."

"You're not going on with that tank?" The question was asked quite unemotionally, so it seemed. He did not answer it. She said:

"If you were a waiter the hours would suit us fine." Outside the children were making rather a wild noise and Longman frowned.

He said, "Aren't they supposed to be at school?"

She replied, "They keep sending them home." But the conversation was not very serious. The Longman children were very bright, all four of them.

He asked, "Why? Aren't they any good?"

"No," she said. "It's not that. It's just that it keeps on being Saturday. Or it did. It did until now."

He squeezed her hand tightly, and then Tate shouted from the stairs. He brought coffee and they apologized for making him do all the work. Longman determined to be cheerful.

He said, "One good thing, I almost forgot. Norman's tapes. Let's take time off," he added more seriously. "Stop the rocking, a little. Steady ourselves with grand music. Let's do that first."

Oonagh nodded enthusiastically, amazed again how well he understood her. Music was the one thing to help at this moment. It could reassure her, and soothe her, as she bridged the gap. Reality could be postponed just once again.

7

If there was something of the otter there was also something of the Lemming, that suicidal mole, about Oonagh Longman. In nine cases out of ten a woman in love finds a best man too. Practically every engagement and every love affair bears this second relationship. The couple form a solid friendship with a third party, ostensibly the man's friend, in fact the woman's second choice. Passion takes her off the ground, but doing so endangers her, runs contrary to her second instinct, security. For this reason she clings to the best man, the safe brother figure whom she books to pick up the pieces supposing something should go wrong. The pattern can be observed any day, but for some reason Oonagh reacted against it, as if she were afraid that the intensity of her passion might be blunted by any sign of precaution. Had she taken the usual woman's step, at this moment, by befriending Tate, she would have been saved some of the most terrible tortures that any modern woman must ever have experienced. But the Lemming in her, the pride in this passion, made it necessary for her to say to herself, "I want this love to win or else disaster - nothing in between, because anything short of ruin as the alternative might temper down the love."

As they listened to the music, therefore, she did not smile at Tate. Instead, she broke in to say, suddenly, "Tate, why didn't you tell me about Sharpey? You're so secretive. I'm not a child."

Tate was confused by the attack, not understanding why it came. "I'm sorry —" he said, shifting in his seat, and Longman, who was sitting above Oonagh, reached forward and put the tips of his fingers on her shoulder, to stop her rocking the boat.

She said, "We should talk. We're just putting it off."

"Ssh."

"What we're not daring to say is that Sharpey's death is directly to do with that tank of yours. Of course it is. Sharpey went on, didn't he —"

Longman was quite severe with her, saying, "Be quiet, darling," but in that severity there shone another face of love which overwhelmed her at once, and she closed her eyes and tipped back her head against his legs. They listened in silence once more.

It must have been about three minutes later, at the end of the second movement, when it happened. There was a crackle on the tape, a muffled sound, a short pause, and then suddenly there was a new noise, a terrifying, loud noise that filled the whole house. It was the distorted noise of pain, the voice of a man insane with terror, stretched on the rack of fear so tautly that his cries were both treble and bestial.

Within a second they were all on their feet. Oonagh stood white and frozen with horror. Tate, too. Longman dashed to the machine, pulled out the lead, and with a final moan the tape came to rest. Nobody moved.

She started on a very low note.

"That was you, wasn't it?"

Longman said, "No."

Her head turned quickly, facing Tate.

"That was him, wasn't it?"

"I don't know, Oonagh, I —"

Back to Longman, her voice higher now.

"That was you, wasn't it? Answer, answer, answer!"

"No, darling."

But she was wild. He did not even have time to curse Norman for wiping a tape inefficiently. She was attacking him hammer and tong with a curious feminine jealous anger, pounding at his chest with her fists, yet with no intention of hurting him. It was as if she had heard a recording of him in bed with some other woman. She was like a glass cracking.

"It *was* you, it *was* you!"

"No."

"It was you," she said more wearily, now.

He grabbed her, took her in his arms and began to comfort her. "Quietly. Promise. That voice wasn't mine. It was poor Sharpey's."

Tate asked, "Is that true?" and Oonagh looked at him daggers, simply because he had interrupted. His fault was in being present. She broke from Longman then and went over to the window. She said quite flatly, about her love affair, "I knew it would end. I absolutely knew it."

Longman could not answer. He looked pale himself now. The noise on the tape seemed to have delayed action. To judge from his face, it seemed he was hearing the screams, still.

Oonagh said desperately, "You're meant to answer me, Longman —" Then suddenly she spun round, and saying, "Oh, for God's sake let's go out," she ran from the room along the landing and slammed the bedroom door.

Slowly, Tate removed the tape from the recorder. He had to plug the machine in before he could wind it off. While he did so, Longman stood over by the fire, his elbows on the high mantelpiece.

Tate guessed the jangle of nerves, nerves like guy ropes pulling tautly in opposite directions, which made up Longman's present stillness and silence; his precarious equilibrium. Tate had known the couple before. They had been relaxed, reassuringly, for twelve years. He did not know directly what passion could do to people, and he was not so wilful as to pretend to himself that this was not passion but a pretence of it. In every movement, in every look, there had been evidence of the appetite that is never satisfied, yet never frustrated. But Tate's secondhand knowledge of passion, taken from all the

books and plays devoted to it, taught him that in excess,
the participants were destroyed by their own wantonness.
There seemed here to be no sign of anything so plush
as wantonness, itself a dark red word. This passion had
a cutting edge, a light blue, sharp arctic edge to it that
alarmed him. It was on a high single note, not langorous
and lingering and rich. It was a paradox of passion,
between Oonagh and Longman. A hectic, austere passion,
a meeting of bare nerve ends, which is to say a nakedness
that Tate could never have imagined in his wildest dream.

Tate did not think it safe or tactful to inquire too
closely into this new intensity in Longman's marriage.
He therefore stuck to inquiries about Sharpey. Fastening
the tape he asked softly:

"Had the old man gone as far as this when you were
working with him?"

"Have you joined MI5?" Longman did not turn
round.

"No."

"I'm sorry, Tate."

Tate shrugged. Longman moved, turned now, and
yawned.

Tate was very observant. He knew what a yawn at
this point might indicate.

He said, "Are you going to faint?"

"Am I?"

Tate said, "Sit down at once. Christ knows what's
going on here —"

Longman sat and lowered his head. He yawned again,
then bent right down, shook his head, and felt better.
Tate stared at him curiously.

"I'm here: one private listening post, if you want
to speak."

Longman nodded his thanks then made a wide gesture
with his big blue-veined hand. "Let's stick to the question
first asked," he said, pulling himself together. "The
answer is 'no'. The old man had not gone as far as
this when we parted. I had been in the tank longer myself.
But nothing like as long as that. I guess that noise indicates

immersion of five hours, minimum. . . . Do you wonder that I about turned and walked out on him? I ran, Tate. I escaped."

"With Oonagh."

Longman did not like it. The question was too close, but Tate was an old friend. He therefore attempted to answer, reaching that same taut steadiness, that calm on the edge of the vortex. Longman seemed to paddle quietly along undisturbed water, and all around was the roar of the fall and the whirlpool that lay only a few hundred yards ahead.

"Love becomes very important when one's scared. It's not simply a case of grabbing the nearest body after you've been starved of sensation. Not only that, even if that's there. One's skin is so tender after the tank, after that torturing physical loneliness - you can't imagine, but the touch of a soft hand across your shoulder feels hot, almost sore, as if the skin were abrased. It also shatters one to the spine. Touch, nobody guessed, is a drug. It stares us in the face, but nobody noticed it before. You can take your morphine, snow, all the rest, their urgency is nothing when you compare it with the reaction to the withdrawal of the oldest connexion in the world - the connexion we call touch. But it's not only that, not with Oonagh. One is so amazed by one's own physical reaction that there comes a second wave of terror, when in reflexion, in bed if you like, one snaps the idea that one has no soul whatsoever. . . . One is, after all, not much more than that vulgar polythene man they sell with the textbooks - inside, a series of pumps and drains, outside, an electric nerve-diagram. Man's vanity, or at least Longman's vanity can't tolerate that. Love - make the leap, Tate, and understand. Love becomes survival."

Tate twigged. He saw the process, and even if he could not imagine the degree, he understood the principle. The step from isolation, to touch, to sex, to screams, to loneliness again, so to love. It made sense. But he could not help asking, "Has it been quite fair to Oonagh?"

"Fair?" The question seemed to bewilder Longman.

It was not that he was an insensitive character. The opposite; he had an exceptional tenderness and strength. But a man expects. A man presumes. Any woman knows that in the strength and naturalness of that presumption lies the male attraction. He shook his head. He said, "I love Oonagh. . . . Fair?" He frowned again. He said, "I think it's fair." Then as if the question bewildered him, almost as if it had been framed in a language with which he was not quite familiar, he chose to switch the subject back, asking, "What has this Major got to say about Sharpey?"

Tate sniffed. "His line couldn't be clearer. Sharpey evidently met the wrong people."

"He was always meeting the wrong people."

"He wasn't always given a brief-case full of fivers."

"A *what*?"

Tate explained. He described his first meeting with Ramrod on the cinder track. He said, "The Major seems to think that adds up. Two plus two make Treason."

Longman groaned. "Lunkheads," he described her Majesty's anti-espionage corps. "Lunkheads! . . . Sharpey? Oh, no, come on. Sharpey as Matahari, come on - You're not believing it?" Tate pouted. Longman stood up, spoke louder, "Have you forgotten the man already?"

Tate was not ruffled. He replied with the truth. "I find it hard to explain: or more accurately, to explain away."

"Maybe . . ." In this sort of argument Longman was a simpler man than many of his colleagues. His loyalty here was secure as a boy's. "But, believe me, there must be an explanation. He was even more of a patriot than he was a pacifist. Of course he wasn't a traitor."

Tate pocketed the tapes. He said, "If you've got any theories you'd better tell them to our Major. That's if you think it's worth while. Sharpey's dead, either way."

Longman shook his head. "What do you take me for? Of course it's worth while."

But continued blasts on the horn of the Lagonda interrupted them, indicating that Oonagh was dressed, downstairs, and ready for the ride.

Tate saw them off, and had to comfort all the children when the Lagonda disappeared. They were furious that they had not been invited. But furious in a heartening, healthy, and extremely noisy way. They had already told their mother and father what they thought about being left behind. Yet, in a curious way, the idea of their parents in the big car, whizzing through the country-side, alone, like nobody else's parents, seemed to excite them. The mirage appealed. The Lagonda was a celestial chariot.

This did not save Tate. He was sharply cross-examined when he offered them chocolate, which they swiftly accepted, but with haughty thanks. Persephone put it quite bluntly.

"Tatty, are you in love with our mother?"

8

They used to drive to a flat field not far from the Round House which marks the junction of the Thames and the old Thames Severn Canal. There were a few poplar trees there, and they would park the car pointing west, looking over open fields to some thick hedges and a copse a mile away. In the evening, when the sun set, the land seemed very narrow and the sky was wide and high and mighty. They sat, this evening as every evening before, feeling that they had never watched the sky before. The wind had dropped, there was some light cumulus overhead at a great height and the blueness of the upper air looked very faint. Soon, the white clouds turned rosier, then gradually altogether more orange. On the horizon, closing over the globe of the sun was a thin, thick, black bank. Birds sang, it seemed, a little too brightly, and flocked and flew too fast as night came in.

Longman and Oonagh did not need to speak. In a curious way they did not need to touch each other, but sat side by side abandoned to each other's company, their faces pale and serious, like two druids, preparing for some savage sacrifice.

Long after, as if explaining her earlier hysteria, as if apologizing for treating Tate badly, Oonagh said, "I don't want to see anybody else: I don't want to hear of anything else. I no longer have the personality with which to present myself."

Longman accepted that, and a while later, he too made his statement. He simply said, with sadness, "You can't escape all the people all the time. That's the gloomy truth about love."

She grasped at once what he was really saying: he was going back to the experiments. Without true evidence —yet still not unreasonably—she felt afraid. When she flung her arms round him and buried her head in his lap saying, "Don't, don't, don't," she was only expressing his own fear which he was determined to control. But he was cold suddenly, his limbs cold, his teeth almost chattering.

"Tell me my motive."

"Adam's motive," she said, bitterly, sitting up. "You're just destroying Eden —"

"That was Eve."

"That came later, I'm sure," she said. "Eve was never afraid to love. That was part of her pride or her wickedness or whatever it was called." She paused. Then, as if struck by a new thought, she continued, "We've gone too far, so the gods will be envious and destroy, and we'll be torn up by wolves. Something like that will happen, and our bodies will be cold carnage lying all over the place. So scared are we by what we've found that you want to destroy it."

"Never. There was no thought of that until I read about Sharpey."

"Guilt for a motive."

"Yes," he admitted.

"That's much what I said."

"If it came off - If I go through and we do find out the whole process of the breakdown and then the building up of the mind, they will say, 'What a brave scientist to undergo all that to find out more about the human brain . . .' I wouldn't dream of it!"

"What exactly do you suppose happened to Sharpey?" It was a question she did not really want to ask and he answered with a sigh.

"I guess . . . But my mind bounces off, now. Tomorrow I'll state it, then try and prove it, I suppose. The Major will imagine that I am doing so to clear Sharpey's name. I won't deny that. It sounds splendid. But that's not my motive. That whole sky says 'Sharpey killed himself, while you two lay with love at each other's throats. Now pay!' If Antony and Cleopatra paid, so must everybody else. In a hundred ways I could say the same thing. 'Guilt for a motive.' I never knew it had such a compelling drive. Even you recognize it. We can tell that from the feebleness of your cry of 'don't' . . . God, I'm cold. Let's go back and put some whisky into blue tumblers - those wedgewood things - and a block of ice, and light music, modern, and a massive box of cigarettes. Drink, smoke, and be still, lest tomorrow we go mad."

But she would not let him start the car. She took his hand and led him; led him quickly, quickly over the bridge and down the path that follows the old canal through willows, and thorns to the mossy patch where the foxes play. They stayed there, until the moon came up. They looked slim and white and pleasantly amazed. Oonagh lay naked in his arms, as if for an eternal span, bathed in Miranda's light.

9

Old soldiers tell the truth to everybody but themselves. That's more or less what makes them square. So when they do try to tell lies they are hopelessly transparent. But to give Ramrod his due, he knew this much about himself, so when he told the lab-boy Norman that he had dropped into "Isolation" merely to look over the tank and recording equipment, both of them instantly heard the lie and neither believed in it.

Ramrod almost blushed, but he shoved through to Lab A with Norman following. As Ramrod paused, and swallowed because the room was more metallic and weird even than the film had suggested, Norman moved ahead and ran up the gantry steps to the top of the huge tank. He was like a cabin boy running about the engine room of some liner that had been sunk and abandoned and lain for years at the bottom of the sea. There was no sound from his steps on the ladder. It was as if the properties of matter had changed: voices did not echo or ring against metal any more. Even Ramrod, straining his imagination, thought "how odd, how odd, how odd". And then he too climbed up to the gantry and the lip of the tank.

Rather unnecessarily, he began, "My brain ticks over slowly." But Norman did not smile. After a pause, therefore, and a little gurgle of discomfort in the lower abdomen, Ramrod boldly continued, "Am I right in thinking that this is merely an extension of the film you showed me, Mister Norman? I mean, is this tank, in effect, the same as Doctor Bonvoubois' abandoned hut in the Arctic?"

Norman said, "It's not for me to answer the scientific inquiries, you understand that? I'm not responsible for what goes on here, nor am I qualified to describe the research work. I'm the lab technician."

Ramrod nodded. "I understand that." He said, "I gather I'm talking to a mere Humphrey Davy, not Michael Faraday," and chuckled, proud of this little compliment.

But Norman did not go for butter. He said, "You're talking to Norman, and Norman, by the by, is my Christian name. I lost my surname when I got my card - lab boys do."

Ramrod laughed at that, a little too loudly as if he wanted to break the gloomy atmosphere of this, Lab A. Norman, rather surprisingly, softened at this point. Underneath what he said now and for the next few moments there seemed to lie an appeal; an appeal which Ramrod was not slow to recognize. Most people want to talk. If this were not true, Ramrod would be cut out of a job. And if there were no Curzon Street, my goodness, it would be difficult to know where he would find another place. In Whitehall the offices are already choc-a-bloc. The spies have got in first.

Unbuttoning, then, Norman said, "On the other hand, if you want the blind to lead the blind, I'll tell you, I think you've got it right. That's exactly what the tank is. Maybe more. It's an extension, a kind of refinement of the dark hut."

Ramrod nodded and took a few steps along the gantry to touch a black rubber frogman's suit which was hung over the side there.

He asked, "They're submerged in this?"

"That's it, and the mask, of course, which I keep in the stores in Lab B. It's got to be cared for properly. Mind, they used to go in naked, at the start. Doctor Longman did. Don't ask me why. But apparently the rubber suit's better. It reduces sensation even more, provided it fits. That one was Sharpey's, poor old goat."

Ramrod recognized the cue, but instinctively did not rise to it first time. Instead he asked some more technical questions and again, swiftly, Norman provided the answers.

"Temperature's always the same - blood heat, same as a bath one's lain in too long. You know, when you can't quite summon up the energy to get out and get cold, drying yourself."

"Indeed I know," Ramrod said enthusiastically. As a bachelor living alone, he knew much about baths. "Now tell me, can the chap in the tank call the outside world?"

"You bet. I'll show you the helmet and mask. Kind of half way between a diver's and a spaceman's, I'd say."

"It has a microphone fitted?"

"Lord, no, we're very primitive in here. He's got a speaking tube that's all, then that leads to a perfectly simple stand-up mike at the edge there, so his voice is carried through to us, in Lab B." He pointed up to an enclosed gallery much like the bridge of a ship, overlooking the tank. Norman continued, "I've got the tapes in there, and he talks all the time, or —" He stopped suddenly.

"Or yells?"

Norman nodded. "Let's say he's in contact all the time. Mind, he doesn't hear a word we say in there. Not that I say much. With Sharpey in this last series, I've been on my own."

"That must have been a big responsibility."

"It scared me stiff." He looked up at Lab B. "Alone in there, with a clock, clear instructions when to take him out, and down here a man on a rack? . . . You give me the Chamber of Horrors, any night."

Ramrod was taking it all in. He pointed now to some cords, hung like nooses, above the tank.

"What are these?"

"Cords."

"That's fairly obvious."

Norman grinned. "You mean 'what for' . . . Sharpey didn't want to lie at the bottom or the side or at the surface, you see. Same principle as the fitting of the rubber suit. With the cords tied, he's kept free but more or less in the middle of the tank, and that way he feels less. Sees nothing, smells nothing because there's damn all to smell except the sweat off his own brow, tastes nothing, unless maybe the salt when he cries; feels the minimum. It's simple enough, isn't it?"

Ramrod nodded solemnly. "It's hard to believe that's all there is to it. You wouldn't think it would be so difficult to have a tepid bath in a dark room."

Norman said, flatly, "You wouldn't, would you? Only two have tried. One's dead, and the other ran away."

Ramrod stopped, and took his cue. He said, slowly, "When I am grilling a witness, I rather like to have a beer in hand. D'you think I could subpoena you to the Kings Arms, private bar?"

"Not only could you subpoena me," Norman said, "but I'd come willingly."

Ramrod, of course, had done much more prep than he disclosed. He was as certain of Norman as you can be about anybody, which did not mean that Norman was the president of the young conservatives. Spies, Ramrod would occasionally admit, with a blush, in his cups, work by sex, nine times out of ten. There was rather a famous anecdote on this very subject. Once, on a security check, visiting a Battalion of the British Army on the Rhine, Ramrod announced to an astonished gathering of officers, "Frankly, gentlemen, I'm on the look-out for queers." It was the last time he opened a lecture that way. But there was the essence of truth. He was not only on the look-out for homosexuals but, more broadly, for people with something to hide, which in the end, has to do with sex. And anyone denying this principle, should do so, please, with forethought and great caution.

Norman's strength lay in his weakness for his fat wife. Oxford seems to be a good climate for marriage. Frankly, his worst problem was to get to work on time, and spy-wise, his most dangerous period was one fortnight annually; the week before she had the baby, and the week after. And even then, a spy could not be certain. Politically, he was solidly, conservatively bolshy. He went on about that in the corner of the pub, with a great relish, enjoying as usual, airing the chips on his shoulder, "When I started, I can tell you, it wasn't beer and skittles. All I did was chase butterfly nuts off a conveyor belt and screwed nothing but wheels on bikes. The real strong monotony in Cowley, and I'm the underdog. So I get out of this by a bit of night school and eventually I get taken as an apprentice technician down in Physical Chemistry. But maybe the butterfly nuts, something, anyway, bends me towards the biological side and, dead crafty, I get a shift into Biochemistry which nobody likes and everybody knows is the most important of the lot. Then one day, when half of Oxford's got Asian 'flu, I creep into Physiology proper, I fasten on to Doctor Longman, get through my Lab Assistant's finals on the Biology side, and then it's High Altitude Physiology with him, until we set up Isolation. And to be perfectly frank, I wish we never had done."

Ramrod had to do little more than buy the beer and use his broad straight shoulders to screen the boy from unwanted eavesdroppers. So the flow continued.

"Like I say, I was the underdog, that's how I felt, and d'you know what I become?" He took a long swig of beer for emphasis. "I become the dog."

Ramrod raised his eyebrows. Norman drank again. He had a surprisingly large capacity, it seemed, for such a slight frame.

"Oh, yes I do. I become the faithful, worshipping, hound-dog, first of Doctor Longman, then next of the Professor, old Sharpey, silly old goat." He added this description again, not coldly, as before, but with considerable emotion. "I'd have done anything for that man. And if I were to meet him outside the lab, he probably doesn't so much as recognize me. There's genius," he said, and then he added, "and there's what a mug I am."

Ramrod encouraged him with talk of loyalty.

"Sure," Norman cut him short. "I see that, and I'm not saying I go with you and your sort, not all the way, but I've checked up on you, I know fine who you are and that's why I'm talking like this. The beer's helping me. Don't think you're screwing it out of me. I want to say this. I *want* to."

Ramrod said he was glad and asked him to continue. He did so very seriously.

"I don't know why he did what he has done. But if you think someone was getting at him, I'll do anything on this earth to help you get one back. Old Sharpey was half in this world and half in outer space, but he was a genius, you could tell. Longman's good but Sharpey was in a different class altogether, on top. What a mind! And he wouldn't have hurt a fly. So shoot. . . . I'll answer your questions."

Ramrod nodded with satisfaction. He already had them in his mind, listed, of course, and numbered properly.

"Did you work with Sharpey until the end?"

"Every experiment."

"Did anybody else come in during these experiments?"

"No one."

"You never left the lab during an experiment?"

"What? With him in the tank? Don't be silly, he had to get out."

"And he used to tell you to take him out?"

"Before, he did. It was worked on the clock. We advanced by quarter, sometimes half hours. It doesn't sound much, but put a bloke in the tank and it's forever. I can tell you time looks silly. The longest I ever kept with him was five hours and the half. It seemed like fifteen years. But when once I did pull him out before the time —"

"Why did you do that?"

"You haven't heard what they say."

"Did you think he was in danger?"

"You mean of dying?"

Ramrod nodded.

"Not that," Norman admitted. "The torture's too bloody subtle for that. The mask continues to work. The bloke continues to breathe. He won't die, even if he wants to. They got him on the rack, that's what it sounds like, and first when you think he's got to bust up and die, it goes the other way. . . . You got to see it. I can't explain all that. But Sharpey thought he was getting somewhere, else he wouldn't have gone on like that. He used to arrive at the torture chamber, hat on, brief-case and brolly - you know - just as if it were the office."

"You have a great admiration for Sharpey?"

"You bet."

"And Longman?"

Norman was caught unawares. He looked into his beer as he said, "Longman's a fair enough bloke."

Ramrod took an uncharacteristic leap ahead. He said, "Come on —" Only that.

Norman put down his beer. "Well - So he is."

"— As a scientist?"

"You can underestimate him as a scientist. Maybe his being American. We all had our doubts. But that lab, the whole thing, the tank, the tapes, all dead simple, that's Longman. He's a 'fixer'. You know what I mean? Half of them, they may manage the equations but ask them to put in a screw and they're lost. Not Longman. He'd do my job better than me, and that's not to say he's lacking on top. He doesn't jump to things, but he gets there better than most of them, only slowly - You should see his handwriting. It's like a child's, and his spelling's worse than mine. When he writes a paper Tate has to half write it for him, but what's there's good. Like in the film. You saw yourself. It was Longman snaps it's not Low Temperature. That's really typical of him. Round the lab, too, he can go on for hours, no panic, endless patience. He used to be on biochemistry, too, trying to list Enzymes - you know, catalyst things, here one minute and gone the next. You can't get a bigger test of an experimentalist than that. It's lovely watching him. Whistling, droning away, like a little boy making a toy aeroplane, all the time in the world. . . . I think I'm saying he's good, really good. Not a genius maybe, but a proper research type, and more strength to his elbow —"

The expression seemed to remind him of his beer. He finished it in one, and Ramrod, without further prompting, went to the bar and had another pint drawn.

With a belch, Norman warmed up again.

"As I say, Longman's fair enough."

"You sound as if you're excusing him."

"I don't know . . ."

"When did he stop coming into Isolation?"

"Two months ago. Mind, I can't blame him for that. Until then he'd done all the nasty part. He wouldn't let the old man into the tank. He was putting himself on the rack week after week while I worked the tapes and the Professor took notes. So don't get me wrong when he said he'd had enough, I was with him, a hundred per cent. But the Professor insists on going on without him."

"Did you see Longman about that?"

"Yep."

"Wouldn't he do anything?"

"He went to the Professor."

"What good did that do?"

"None."

"You mean he went on?"

"Harder than ever."

"Did Longman know that?"

"That's the whole point. He knew damned well. I saw him again more than once. He just said there was nothing he could do, and then he didn't even see me. Well, by then, this thing - this picnic lark, you've heard - had started with Oonagh."

"I haven't heard."

"Then it's not for me to tell you. I'm not the bloke to criticize. But his performance becomes ridiculous," he added, angrily. "Love's one thing, but —" Then he stopped himself. "Anyway, he wasn't going to do anything other than spend twenty-four hours of the day with that Oonagh. So the Professor goes on, and I'm not going to leave him."

"Why didn't you appeal to somebody else?"

"Who?"

"Say, Calder."

"Oh, Major, come on - what the hell does Calder know, except the ladder? Tell Calder, he'd have Sharpey invalided out and grab the Chair himself."

"What about Tate?"

"Tatty?" Norman smiled. "He's a boy. Tatty couldn't do anything. He's like the rest of them: all grey matter and crossword puzzle. You should see him when Oonagh's anywhere near. He blushes at the thought of her smiling. Mind, they're all the same with her. Me too, come to that."

"I haven't met Mrs. Longman," Ramrod admitted.

"Whoo," Norman said. The beer was to cool him down. "Four kids, but all the same . . . She's a knock-out. See her at a lab party, they're all round her. Grabbing, if they dared." He extended his hands in a gesture which seemed to indicate a clutch at her lower half. Evidently it reminded him. "Yeah," he said, dizzily. "It's high time I got back home. Past time, I'd say."

PART TWO

10

Breakfast time in North Oxford is worse than elsewhere in the country. Here, the children have to get to school but the fathers can take their time. Besides, there are so many children. Conditions in the Longman household, at half past eight or a quarter to nine on the following morning were chaotic, indeed.

Persephone, like every elder sister in the world, felt obliged to take over responsibilities which her parents were shirking.

She said, "I can tell you quite clearly we are going to be late again, unless some people get their coats and hats on bloody-quick." The last was delivered as a kind of chanting threat which put Penny into a rage, and almost made her cry. These two were in the front hall.

The boys were still at breakfast, where Longman, too, was finishing his coffee and changing out of his slippers at the same time. He also felt resentment at Persephone's bossiness.

"I'm coming," he said rattily, as if he too had to be buttoned into his coat.

His eldest son did not like milk, but his wife liked his elder son to drink his milk.

"Finish it," Oonagh said. She was surprisingly firm with them.

"I hadda pinta."

"Liar."

"I hadda pinta yesterday."

"You finish it," Oonagh warned, and Penny drifted back with her school mac buttoned wrongly, so her stomach looked enormous. She said, "Mother, you mustn't force him to milk. That way you could mix him up badly, inside."

Even Longman looked up at that one. But Oonagh was not going to be distracted.

"Finish it," she said, and in three resentful gulps, it was done.

"Good boy."

From the dishmaster which was in the corner Oonagh said, "Hurry darlings," as if it were any morning in May. But as the children returned to the hall Longman crossed to her for a moment and she held his hand.

He said, "School for me today too. Remember?" And he searched her face, but she would say nothing. She stared at him solemnly and he said, "Don't make me late."

Among the children, Penny did most of the talking. She returned to the kitchen, took her father's hand and said, "Do you think algebra is essential for girls, Daddy?"

He thought it out. But Oonagh answered, "Essential", at once.

Persephone called from the hall. "Daddy, have you got your bicycle clips?" And by the table, Peers knocked over a packet of cornflakes. Paul and Penny made a dive for the free plastic gift inside. Persephone shouted "Come on", Oonagh shouted, "Persephone, do not shout!" And Peers, abandoning the chaos of the cornflakes, went to his tricycle and took some cycle clips off the handlebars. His mother, spotting them, grabbed them from him before they got lost. But silence was at last suddenly imposed by a sharp knock on the door.

"Who on earth could that be?" Oonagh asked.

"Search me. Registered post?" Longman suggested.

Persephone said, "The Secretary of the noise abatement society, I shouldn't be surprised."

"Or the schools inspector," Paul said.

"Do shut up, children," Oonagh said. She was straining to hear, as Longman answered the front door. It seemed to be a stranger.

"Perhaps the police about speeding —"

"Shut up, P."

Longman was saying, "What can we do for you?"

Coming through from the kitchen to the hall, Oonagh heard the reply.

"My name is Hall, Major Hall."

"Ah!" Longman said slowly. "The man from the ministry."

Inside there was complete quiet now.

Ramrod could not have missed the hostile edge in Longman's voice. The children certainly had not. In the silence there was a great air of hostility.

"If you could spare five minutes," Ramrod said.

"As you know, I've already spared five weeks," Longman answered drily, and swung back the door. "You'd better come in."

"But Daddy, we'll all get black marks again," Persephone said. "It's nearly nine."

Longman frowned. He said, "I'll speak to your teacher."

"Promise?"

"Yes . . . Get them ready, Otter —"

"We are ready."

"Are the bikes pumped?"

Oonagh said, "Come on, children, we'll check the tyres," and knowing full well this was a mere excuse, they obeyed her, looking at Ramrod with great suspicion from the corners of their eyes.

Penny said, "A bailiff, I bet," and was told not to try to be funny.

Longman indicated the room that had been the dining-room, which had a wigwam in one corner. He did not try to explain it away. But at the last moment, as he was about to close the door, his son Peers cycled up to take a close look. Longman hesitated, then beckoned him closer. Pulling him off the tricycle, he carried him into the dining room, telling Ramrod, "If you don't mind, I'd like a witness. A fellow civilian."

Peers seemed to like the idea. He stood about the settee, while his father half sat and half leant on its arm. All the time his father talked Peers played around with his pockets or the buttons on his sleeve. Longman soon forgot him, but continued absently to touch him and play with him as if he were a puppy not a child, lolling about in the patch of sun.

Ramrod was a well trained man. He did not beat about the bush.

"I believe you were a close friend of Professor Sharpey's?"

"You know it." Longman looked at Peers, and said, "The man knows it."

Ramrod was not put off. "You worked with him on Isolation?"

"For a limited period."

"What limited it?"

Longman turned to his son and vaguely answered him. "A strong sense of panic on Daddy's part."

"Doctor Longman, I know of Professor Sharpey's activities in London, so obviously I want to be sure that no ends are left untied. Tell me, did he, during the last few months have - what shall we say? - any *surprising* visitors to the lab?"

Longman dropped his head. At last, and again to Peers, he said in a low voice, "Oh my God, listen to the man." He turned back to answer Ramrod. "Tell me, does it ever occur to Majors that they may be meddling in affairs about which they understand absolutely nothing?"

But Ramrod was at his best when his opponent's temper rose. He said calmly, " 'Majors' duties are clearly outlined. If bewildered they report back to their Colonels. The reasons which bring me here are quite simple. Professor Sharpey was dealing with what are defined for Majors as . . . undesirable people."

"Fine," Longman said, standing up and forgetting Peers now. "Fine, fine. So he qualifies for the rogues gallery, sub-section treason."

"I have proof."

"Major, you're a tonic - 'Do this, you're a patriot - Do that, you're a traitor.' "

Ramrod was at his best. "Obviously," he said. Then as Longman moved to the other end of the room he continued, "I understand your feelings —" but was at once interrupted.

"You understand nothing. Nothing at all." Longman moved back to the Major. "Look, I've worked a little on Isolation. We have a tank —"

But then Persephone appeared at the window.

"Daddy —"

"- A perfectly ordinary tank."

"Daddy!"

Longman came to. "What is it, darling?"

"We want Peers."

Longman nodded absently. "Oh, sure. You have him." And again he spoke to Ramrod. "But drop into this tank, one man —"

"Daddy, out here! We want him out here! Please pass him out."

Longman took it in slowly. Then slowly obeyed. The picture which Norman had painted of the lonely experimentalist with blanket concentration had been very accurate. If Longman had been asked what he was passing out of the window, and why, he would not have been able to answer. And though he now spoke with great emotion, his opponent, Ramrod, who had done his prep, was moves ahead.

Longman ran on, "Drop this man in, leave him there in the tank for a while and he dissolves, mentally, I mean, dissolves until he is reduced to a soul-less, will-less thing; not a man, but a kind of sea anemone. How's that for an eerie hypothesis?"

Ramrod had heard all this but he played with great care. Early in the morning he had risen from his lone, unlevel bed and reappreciated. Especially he had concentrated on breaking down "*Object,* to defend the Queen and her Commonwealth." He had noticed that he was no longer primarily interested in Sharpey's deflexion. You can't lock a dead man in a tower. He was certain, anyway, that the old man had committed some treasonable act. He was interested, of course, in the possibility of other traitors in the camp, but Sharpey's lonely habits and temperament, as confirmed by Norman, suggested to him that he probably worked on his own. His first interest was therefore the nature of the information which had passed. It suited him very well that Longman, in his simplicity, should batten on the idea of defending the old man's name. All Ramrod had to do was pooh-pooh this enough to make Longman determined to return to the lab and carry the experiment through to its bitter end. That this might be a distressing process was not relevant, because Ramrod could do the most dangerous thing that any man can do. He could wear blinkers. Recognize, therefore, what Longman did not recognize in this just Pontius Pilate with the controlled schizophrenia; in this kind, dispeptic British bachelor, recognize the villain of this piece. He played it beautifully.

"I have in fact seen your tank, but you can only be guessing —" He allowed himself to be interrupted.

"Major, please. Faraday was only guessing, at the start. All I'm suggesting, as politely as I can, is that you might take a closer look at what happens to the man in the tank. Consider what may have happened to Sharpey, before you close the book on him and file it under 'T' for traitor."

Ramrod did not seem to be convinced. He said, "It's one thing to discuss a theory —"

"So it is." Longman, predictably, grew more violent in his defence of Sharpey. "I admit I'm going along untracked country, because somewhere back along the track X marks the spot where I fell by the wayside. But what I mean to do is to demonstrate to you that a man can change in the tank. He can come out no longer responsible for his actions. If I can prove this,

then you can click your heels and report back, 'Dear
Colonel Bogey, we got it wrong. Spies ain't what they
used to be.' "

Ramrod pushed it once again.

"I understand your wanting to protect Sharpey's name,
but you shouldn't forget that I hold a great deal of
evidence against him."

"You bet! Neatly filed. But if my guess is right, Major,
Sharpey's file should have been closed a month ago
when he - poor, dear, old, dedicated brave ass - sunk
himself alone in that tank for far too long. A new file,
labelled Z for Zombie, should have been begun. And
Z for Zombie, not S for Sharpey should be filed alongside
Guy Fawkes and all the other traitors. . . ."

"You're very eloquent. But how can you prove this?"

"By putting somebody in the tank."

Ramrod raised his eyebrows.

"This time I'm not falling by the wayside," Longman
said, and Ramrod knew he was there. As he protested,
but mildly again, Oonagh came in.

She said, "Darling, if you're going to take the children
you must go at once." Her voice was so well controlled
that she sounded flat and weary.

Longman nodded. "I'm coming."

In the hall, she said, "If you want, I'll take them."

"No, we've finished anyway." He introduced her
then to Ramrod, who shook hands, briefly.

Longman said, "We've got a date at the Labs."

"This morning?"

"As soon as I've delivered this lot," he said, referring
to the children. It was very noticeable how Ramrod's
blinkers had not let him see Peers. Now he was blind
to Oonagh and the other children. He would not have
recognized them had he met them, that afternoon, in
the street.

Longman said, "Where did I put my clips?" and the
children shouted to Oonagh, who brought them, almost
lethargically.

"I've got them."

"Come on then, children," Longman said, and he checked three as they streamed out in the garden. Ramrod, raising his hat, also left, down the garden path. Peers was back on his tricycle, in the hall.

"Clips," was all Longman said to his wife. And she handed them to him, but held on to them for an instant as if to pull him back. He waited for her to let go, not daring to say anything to her. Then she let go and he ran to get his bicycle which was a girl's one, anyway. He and the children cycled in Indian file, all the way to school.

Oonagh, in the kitchen, smoked a cigarette and Peers with that uncanny telepathy not of his alone, but of all children's, went and held on to her skirts.

11

Tate was demonstrating to some of the third year men on respiration again. They were using a running machine similar to the one used, ten years before, by Dr. Roger Bannister, who used to run for Oxford on the track and occasionally, for physiology, on the machine in the lab. The principle was that the man had to keep up with the rollers under his feet. The faster they went, the more energy he expended. The students were checking the rate of breathing and the body temperature, making the same sort of remarks to the poor bloke on the rollers that are made every year. Tate did not even hear them, now, and he was standing apart from the experiment when Longman appeared at the door. Tate strolled out to the polished corridor.

Longman did not look as casual as his invitation sounded.

"If you'd care to come down, I'm going to take myself a bath."

Tate stared at him carefully. "Isolation?"

Longman nodded. "I know what I'm doing. I can't force you to come."

Tate put his hands in the pockets of his white coat. He recognized the motive "guilt" by one look at Longman's face, and decided not to argue. He stared back at his students who were laughing at some new sally.

He said, "They'll play with that thing for hours." Then he wandered back, had a word with the most responsible of the students, and left it at that.

The two men wandered past Calder's office and to Tate's unspoken question, Longman gave a negative reply. It was sunny outside.

Suddenly Tate asked, "How long are you going in for?"

"All the way."

"Meaning?"

"Meaning as much as I can tolerate *physically*, or until the pattern of behaviour starts repeating itself. It could do that."

"What are we going to do with you when we take you out?"

"Treat me like a returned POW, with love and care and red meat."

Tate did not comment. They approached the horrid little hut. "It's a bit of a chance, isn't it?"

Longman grinned. "I like that!" he said. "I thought Englishmen packed up that understatement talk in '45. It's murder, that's what it is. But man's obstinacy, in this case, is complete. In I go, and in I stay, Tatty, until we know what the hell does happen."

"Isolation" had a yale lock on its door and as they stood in front of the "Positively no entrance" sign, Longman fished in his pocket for the key. A second before he fitted it in the lock, he looked over his shoulder at Tate, and asked,

"D'you know what fear over a long period does? It exhausts. It doesn't come and go. It permanently haunts."

Then he opened the door, and in they both went. The corridor was dusty and dull like the corridor of any other hut, but it stopped Longman. The musty smell almost overpowered him there and then, and as he stood stock still, Tate softly closed the door. They could hear voices coming from Lab B.

Tate said, "It sounds as if the military have anticipated us," and Longman nodded then moved forward. It was necessary to climb a few wooden steps to get into Lab B, but inside, there was nothing exceptional about the room. It looked much like a projector room, with a highly complicated recorder with several special attachments, instead of a projector. The light was from a small window at the side and the sun shone against a wall masked with sheets of sound-proofing material which looked like a Meccano board. The place was as untidy and undusted as any other lab, and tucked under the table there were boxes of papers, tapes, wires, valves, and other apparatus which Norman had been meaning to sort out for six months.

Norman was at his most serious and enigmatic. No one could have missed his attitude with regard to Longman. It was more of embarrassment than hostility. Yet he still could not hide his pleasure at seeing him again.

Ramrod was behaving like a guards' officer. He had picked up a rule, to act as a swagger stick and with it he tapped the dashboard of the huge recorder.

He said, "I can't quite understand why we have such a very complicated recorder."

As Longman and Norman were talking together, awkwardly, by the window, Tate felt obliged to answer.

"Because we record just about everything we can. Not only what he says but his pulse rate, blood pressure, body temperature —"

"Why do you want all these?"

Tate looked up at him. He said, quietly, "To check if the gentleman is still alive. . . . Clear?"

In Lab A, they followed Longman, watching him

as he stepped nervously and very slowly towards the tank. He said nothing as he walked up to the gantry, and looked into the big bath which was slowly filling with water. The others stayed below. Longman touched the rubber suit, looked down at them, looked back in the bath, up at the noose-like cords, then slowly he descended the steps again, and sat on the second last one.

He said, "As you see, we've got a military man present, so we'll go about this little patrol into unknown country in a proper military fashion." That was said quietly, humourlessly, and coldly, but he perked up now, and speaking heartily, he saluted and began. "Sah! . . . One and A, Information? Is the equipment checked? Norman, take two paces forward."

"I checked it."

"Excellent!" Longman began to walk about. He was as nervous as a cat: stiff and stretchy with nerves. "Two and B —" But the act seemed to fade away for a second as he looked round again. He said, "It will be noisy in here, noisy . . ." and then he turned to Ramrod. "Nasty, isn't it? Strictly Frankenstein country. . . . Only it happens to be fact." Slowly he was gathering strength and authority. He seemed to be growing in front of them. He snapped his fingers. "Cigarette, please, Norman, cigarette. . . . It isn't pleasant in the tank, Major - Is the duplicate tape checked?"

"All checked," Norman said.

"Two and B, then - what is it, Major? Object?"

" 'Intention' actually."

" 'Intention' actually. . . . Good. Then let's frame it." He thought for a second and then said quite swiftly, "To find out what happened to the man who went into the tank while his colleague went on picnics."

None of them dared interrupt now. Behind, the note of the water filling the tank grew deeper, as the level approached the top.

Longman coughed as he smoked, then recovered himself. "Method — Today's schedule, then, is to take one

Longman, dissolve him, and if he behaves in a new and dotty way, then present him to the Major here. . . . That done, in a retreat to be designated and told to Lieutenant Tate here, Longman will be handled with much care, always accompanied, until he is readjusted - until he is himself again. He will then be returned to his wife and family, scientist and people's hero. . . ."

Having said that, he paused for a second, then suddenly rushed from the room. They heard his steps as he ran down the corridor, then the banging of the door. Ramrod for a second, followed him, then turned back to the others.

"Where's he going?" he asked.

"To be sick," Tate said flatly. "It isn't pleasant in the tank, Major."

For a second the blinkers seemed to fail. Ramrod said, "I suppose he knows what he's doing?" and rather savagely, Tate said, "If he knew precisely, he wouldn't have to do it at all. Isn't that the point?"

They wandered back, then, to Lab B, where Norman had brewed some coffee, but only a few moments later, Norman went to turn off the taps. "Automation," he commented drily, "I do it all."

Longman was already in Lab A, stripped naked, climbing into the sinister rubber suit. He was at the bottom of the gang-steps and Norman looked down at him, solemnly.

Longman said, "You'd better close the shutters, son, lest we shock the neighbours."

Norman came down, and did as he was told. There were two overhead lights in the big room but these seemed very dull. The two men were mere dim shadows as they climbed on to the gantry. Longman was humming now, flatly, timelessly, "Oh my darling Clementine" as Norman helped him fix the rubber clamps round his biceps, and attach the cords. He bent down and tied his ankles similarly. They exchanged no words.

Longman put on the big helmet and Norman checked the seals, the mask, the speaking tube. When he had done so they stared at each other for a second, then with a gesture, Longman dismissed him.

Norman went down the steps to the door, closed it, then closed the second sound-proofed door. He waited ten seconds, and from Lab B he heard the splosh recorded there as Longman immersed himself. He therefore switched off the lights marked "Lab A, House" on the dial in the corridor. Then he stepped up into Lab B, where Tate had already started the two tape recorders. Both were in order. Longman's voice, recorded on the two sets of tapes, was also perfectly audible in Lab B. To begin with they did not even bother to close the windows or the door. It was only necessary to do that later, when the sounds became too disturbing.

Longman just said, from the tank, "I once talked to a detective who broke a very tough gang. Before he questioned the key witness he made him take off all his clothes and simply sat and stared at him for the first hour. Horrible. . . . He ought to have been dismissed from the force. Or maybe the Major doesn't think so."

There was a pause, then, during which Ramrod settled down in a cane chair by the window. Tate and Norman checked and recorded Longman's pulse, blood pressure, temperature, and also noted the time. The pulse rate was extremely high. The temperature a touch above normal. Blood pressure, normal. Longman's voice came in again.

"What about the physiology of fear, eh? We know that fear can raise the body temperature. I suppose that's what makes the surface of the skin seem so tender and so cold. . . . Hey, diddle, diddle. . . ."

In Lab B Norman adjusted the loud-speaker, reducing the volume slightly.

"The cat and the fiddle. . . . After all, it's only a warm, nearly warm bath."

The three of them listened intently, Norman and Tate both smoking, Norman finishing his cup of cold coffee.

"And here am I, Henry Laidlaw Longman, graduate and doctor of the University of California, LA, the bride in the bath. It takes such hours. One feels apprehensive now. It's very dark. Feels like stretching one's limbs. Like waiting to run a cross-country race . . . in the middle of the night."

12

A report was made of the experiment, to go along with the tapes, but also to be published, at the government's discretion. Longman called it "The Report for Colonel Bogey", when he saw it, long, long after. It was signed both by Ramrod and Tate, but as Ramrod composed it, the style can be imagined. Numbered and methodical, it understated every horror, but missed nothing. It tallies closely with several others read later at scientific conferences held in America on the effects of the reduction of sensation. Longman, who was not of course named in the report, seemed to go through four distinct stages. While the tapes recording other similar experiments may, on first hearing, seem utterly different, there is a frightening similarity. The imagery, for each man, is different, the things he says, the way he expresses them, but the process of disintegration, the road to ruin, so to speak, is always the same. It is our vanity, perhaps, which is most hurt by this discovery. The possibility of courage or strong faith is ruled out. The soul turns out to be a common metal; it has the same properties for all; its dissolution is merely a question of technique. The technique learnt, the process is ineluctable. The rack and the rubber truncheon can be put away. They are obsolete now.

The first general stage, after half an hour of nervousness, and in Longman's case, an accompanying facetiousness, can be termed *Irritation*. Before reaching it, about one hour and five minutes in, Longman went through a spell of apathy, even boredom, but this was not recorded in other, later experiments and probably could be accounted for by his behaviour before entering the tank. In other words he was so intensely and unusually keyed up, before being submerged, that the reaction had to come. The rope of his nerve fibres was pulled too tight not to slacken for a spell. When it did, he grew depressed, saying that he knew the experiment stood little chance of proving anything, and admitted to feeling very tired. He yawned on several occasions, and it was after a long, exaggerated yawn that he seemed to arrive at *Irritation*. Quite suddenly, then, he became abusive, sometimes comically, sometimes childishly, sometimes downright angry.

"Knees up, knees up, knees up!" he shouted. "Knees up, Mother Brown!" and he began to thrash about the water with furious energy, shouting something like forty times, in phase with some sort of physical jerks which could not be seen, but might be assumed to be a sort of pedalling movement, first "Knees up!" then "Bloody stupid damned waste of time. . . . Blood-dy stupe-id damn-ned waste-of time — Blood — dy — stupe . . . etc." Then, after several sequences of this sort, spread over half an hour, he finished with a huge raspberry noise, and the words, "Come in and call it a day, you stupid fat bitch!" - Words, Ramrod added, assumed to be addressed to the mythical Mother Brown - Brown, spelt in the report, incidentally, with an "e", as Mother Browne, but this perhaps betrays a quirk in Ramrod's psychology, not in Longman's.

In another hour he had reached a long, curiously lazy melancholy state, which lasted about three hours. During the course of it any signs of self-consciousness, any awareness that somebody else was listening to him, now disappeared. He became totally disorientated not only within the tank, but with regards to the tank. By the end of the period, in fact, there was nothing to suggest that he even knew that he was submerged. It was a stage leading up to considerable anguish, but at the time his voice, very often, was the voice of a man enjoying considerable sensual pleasure. He began by opening his fingers and rushing his hand through the water. In spite of the thickness of the glove, he could feel something when he did this and for a long time he clung to this single, not unpleasant sensation, much as a child, or grown-up for that matter, might hang his hand over the side of a punt for hours on end, feeling the gentle force of the current passing by.

After this had continued for half an hour, he began to say things which suggested, at first, then confirmed, that his body image was subject to wild changes. In other words he suddenly believed that his fingers were the size of telegraph poles, standing like stakes in the middle of a huge torrent which he associated with the Missouri. He had evidently known the river as a boy. From the fingers, to the arms, to the other parts of the body; he was sometimes the size of Tom Thumb, sometimes as big as a tower. The changes did not seem to alarm him. Indeed, he often laughed, saying, "my toe is getting bigger and bigger, and bigger. It's like a piece of liquorice: a bar of liquorice, a strip of liquorice. . . . Long, black and stretchy. . . . It stretches miles and miles and miles and miles and miles, now. . . . Miles."

It was no surprise to the experimenters when the search for sensation moved from the limbs to parts more directly sexual. The changing body images gradually edged towards erotic hallucination. Several times he called for his wife, or for particular parts of her, and it would be romantic if it could be reported that the sexual images were all connected with her. But it would be quite inaccurate. Not that he called for anybody else. It seemed that starved of sensation from the outer world, the surface of the skin itself grew a sensitivity quite beyond normal experience. By movement in the water alone, and as far as could be ascertained, by astonishingly little movement, he could experience heights of sensual pleasure, leading to a series of orgasms. These were not apparently

associated with any imagined figure, of Oonagh or any
other woman, man or beast. The sensation, when experienced, was intense and enough in itself. The pleasure,
therefore, paradoxically, was conceived in abstract terms,
perhaps more like the pleasures of those drugs which
induce abstract, kaleidoscopic dreams. He was not,
however, very articulate at this time, and in the report
Ramrod hedged this whole second period with qualifica-
tions. "It is thought" and "It could be suggested" pepper
the pages devoted to it.

Several times, during the long erotic sequence, he
was silent altogether and probably blacked out, which
is to say fell into what we would ordinarily call "a
few moments of dreamless sleep", although these terms
can hardly be used in the context. The lines between
sleep, dream, hallucination, and consciousness cannot
yet be defined. But Lethewards, he sank, until at last
he seemed to be so exhausted that he had grown numb.

It was as if he preferred now to ignore any tiny sensation
which he could experience by movement. He lay utterly
still, utterly starved of those five sensations which keep
us, or some of us, more or less sane. This quiet after
the shattering, erotic storm of sensations had an eerie
effect. On the tape there is a low moan, then a long,
long silence, as if the wind has dropped in the wasteland
of his mind.

Then, all of a sudden, silence was broken by a little
sobbing, whining sound. He said, quite clearly, "Please,
please, honestly - It's not fair. It isn't. Please let me out.
Honestly, it's not fair." It was a direct appeal, it seemed,
to his torturers, and it too was repeated at intervals, many
times, finally in an almost emasculated, strangled little
voice, as if he had completely lost confidence in himself
as a man. He had returned to being a child, locked in
the nursery cupboard, and in long, childish gusts, he
wept and wept.

Panic was the third stage. Panic reminiscent of the
menagerie that is on fire. He yelled and thrashed and
howled and moaned without break for moments on end,
during a period of about two hours. It was the voice

of the trapped monkey, the action of the wasp beating again and again against the pane of glass. It had been early in this stage that Sharpey had been lifted from the tank, and some of the noises Longman made were inseparable from the old man's voice on the Sibelius tape. When pain and panic are extended this far there can be no identity. The noise is literally closer to the monkey house than to man.

13

Spies, it has been noticed, work on sex. It was at this point, towards the end of the third stage, when the monkey was becoming too exhausted to cry out any more, that Ramrod, in Lab B, rose from his chair and began, thoughtfully, even purposefully, to walk up and down the narrow little room. The military mind had moved. For Ramrod was a well-trained man.

He knew, for instance, about hypnosis, and he knew as an agent what a snare and delusion it is. As a mental therapy, even as a very special sort of anaesthetic, hypnosis has its uses. As a show, on the stage, it is a sensation, but it is nothing like such a powerful weapon as the showman often suggests. It only scratches the surface. It does not begin to bend the mind. Under hypnosis a middle-aged lady may stand nimbly and unashamedly on her head, and out of the trance, shortly afterwards, she may still be subject to suggestions implanted in her mind. The showman can pull out his handkerchief and the lady will burst out laughing, which is good for the showman's pocket, and fun for the audience, even if some may doubt if it is the right sort of fun, or the right sort of audience. But the idea of full confession, and subsequent indoctrination, under hypnosis, is strictly for the Bulldogs, beyond the widest bonds of possibility. Anyway, the subject in all but the rarest cases, has to co-operate, and even when he is prepared to co-operate it is not always possible for him to fall under the spell. All this, Ramrod had learnt and fully understood.

But the more he heard recorded from Lab A, the more certain did he become that the information worth £1000 had nothing to do with space flight. It was definitely mind-bending country, and Ramrod now clearly remembered the last time when he had heard a man weeping like a child in this disturbing manner, then break into a complete animal panic.

The case - and he remembered neither the name, the nationality, the race, nor the reason, because Ramrod was a trained man, and the blinkers thick - the case had occurred during interrogations in the middle east. A colleague of Ramrod's had succeeded in breaking one of the toughest members of perhaps the best-intentioned, best trained, and toughest underground armies that this century has known. He did so fundamentally without torture, though with plenty of suggestion of it.

The subject was confined in a small dark room and interrogated, night and day, at short intervals for many many days and at no time was it possible for him to sleep for longer than three hours at a time. He lost all idea of time as he was never permitted to know whether it was night or day. Suddenly the questioning ceased. The man then remained in complete darkness, in solitary confinement for some weeks. All this was routine. The genius lay in the final twist. The prisoner began to tap on a certain pipe that ran through his dungeon. Hearing this, the interrogator had the idea to echo the tap. For some days the prisoner could not know if he was hearing merely an echo of his own scratchings, the sound of rats, or the sound of another prisoner. At last, one night the interrogator took the initiative and began the tapping

- which, incidentally, was quite random and meaningless, for both prisoner and interrogator, throughout. The prisoner at once tapped back. Contact had been made and on that contact with another human being, the prisoner now survived. He did so, for eight days, strengthening not weakening during the time, all his hope depending on this single contact with some other tortured man. Then the interrogator stopped tapping. Forty-eight hours later the weeping began. Fifty-seven hours later, the panic started. Fifty-seven and a half hours later the interrogator had the information which he required.

But the difference here, between the man in solitary confinement and Longman, was in the time. There was in fact a direct relationship. Longman had been reduced in as many hours as it took months to break down the other man. Ramrod paced up and down a little more excitedly.

The reports from Korea, Vietnam, and other areas were Ramrod's bedside reading; these and the Golden Treasury. He knew very well the process of interrogation, breakdown, discipline, reassurance, indoctrination, and enrolment. He did not believe that the process was as successful or as extensive as some American observers suggested, but that it did happen, in a limited way, was beyond question. But one of the known things about the process was that it took individual tuition, and more important, it took time. Moreover, the depths of the indoctrination were always being questioned. They were not easily measurable. How deep a Christian, or a communist can a man become? And there was a school of thought which suggested that if you simply gave these indoctrinated men plenty rest, plenty exercise, and some good steaks they then returned to "normal" in next to no time. Ramrod began to chain-smoke. He already saw the goal ahead, but he determined to come to it slowly. It need hardly be added, that in pursuing these thoughts he did not remember Oonagh or her children. He had hardly seen them. They were the other side of the blinkers.

Longman, meantime, in the tank, had slipped into

the fourth stage, the comfort and the blessing of hallucination. His mind, in complete isolation, invented its own images. It is as if the imagination comes to the rescue, and whether this can be counted as a defence of sanity or the first onslaught of madness it is hard to tell. He had been in the tank nearly seven hours, and now for a while he vanished into a world of his own, cloudy, coloured, abstract, and rolling - a cotton-wool world, a dark cathedral moving around him; an endless, comforting womb. The few things he said concerned comfort and visual excitement, as if he had never been so safe before and never known such colours. The stage is called *Mescaline* as the images seem to be similar to those seen by someone under the influence of this, least dangerous drug. The "cathedral" feel of which Longman talked is, however, separate and, Ramrod guessed, not unconnected with his general exhaustion.

As these more reassuring sighs came through to Lab B, Norman and Tate both relaxed a little, and drank more coffee, but Ramrod still continued to pace. He was rolling to the inevitable conclusion. The test must be a measurable indoctrination of some sort. To begin with, Ramrod thought of this in terms of a change of fundamental belief. In other words, if they now whispered some religious or political manifesto in Longman's ear, he might later defend and act according to the maxims in it. But then as he paced and re-examined his own laborious thought processes, he realized that he was talking here in muddled terms. Belief is not measurable, even in terms of subsequent action. Baffled, Ramrod reappreciated, starting at the very beginning, "If a man has all his sensations reduced . . ." and he stopped in his tracks. He need never stray from sensation. The indoctrination could be entirely devoted to reduction of sensations. Ramrod grew excited as he put the proposition to Tate. He talked with the direct, dynamic vigour of a man in blinkers. His theory was perfectly simple. Sexual attraction is clearly controlled by the senses - all five of them, sight, smell, touch, taste, and sound. If these - not the vague "mind" - but these essential senses by which we live, and on whose evidence we make our first judgements - if these could be tampered with, then indeed a thousand pounds was underpayment, and the phrase Sharpey had used had horrifying reality. Here were the first experiments in the physics of the soul.

14

Perhaps it is too hard to call Ramrod the villain of the piece. Perhaps, after all, the villainy of inaction is more despicable than action taken for conscious ends, whatever they are.

Tate, for reasons he did not have the guts to recognize and inspect, simply went along with the blinkered Major. That he would not have done so without ulterior motive is surely true. But at the time his self-deception was complete. There was a thick blanket hiding him from his own longings, which were not to be uncovered for some months. Now he merely accepted the position as Ramrod's assistant in a highly important classified experiment. Norman was pale and silent, but it was not for him to interfere. So they moved to the cross-examination, which was run on the oldest lines, with two interrogators, one sympathetic, the other cruel. It is of course the sympathetic one who finds out most, or alternatively plants most in the subject's mind. Tate, with his nice face and comforting low voice, did it very well.

Norman stayed in Lab B, while the pair of them moved into Lab A, taking with them a lamp fitted up on a rod and bracket which worked like a rough home-made "Anglepoise". This they put on the table, plugging it

into the power point a few feet inside the door. Then
they switched it on and closed the lab door.

The light did not shine anywhere near the tank, but
it was bright and, of course, to lesser extent, it lit up
the whole room, not only the table on which it was at
first directed. But Longman by this time must have closed
his eyes. There was no change in his behaviour. He
was still lying in the comfort of his rolling dark cathedral.

Tate, according to Ramrod's instruction, now readjusted
the light so that it would shine brightly on Longman when
they put him in the chair in front of the table. Ramrod's
chair was placed directly opposite. Tate, as in the Bonvoubois examination, was going to sit on the table close
to Longman, to reassure him.

When the simple equipment was in place, they looked
round the room and swallowed their fear. The blazing
spotlight had changed the haunted ship into a nightmare
torture chamber. The metal and the gantry looked shiny
and dark, like black ice. Curious, strong shadows stretched
to walls and ceilings. It was as if they were surrounded
by huge thin guards with tentacles and spider's limbs.

Ramrod nodded and they proceeded to the tank. Pulling
the cords gently, first, they brought this black shape, this
thing that was Longman, to the surface, then they hauled
him to the side. He did not complain. He said absolutely
nothing, as if dead, but there was none of the stiffness
that goes with the corpse. On the contrary, he was completely supple, and when at first they tried to lift him
out - Tate at his knees, and Ramrod scooping under
his back and shoulders - his head fell right back as if
there were no muscles in his neck. They let him drop
again, then supporting head and arms as well, they heaved
him, with difficulty, on to the gantry, and comically,
he folded up, landing in a heap. They had supported
him enough to prevent the fall hurting him, but for a
moment they were bewildered by this physical problem.
In his wet rubber suit he was very slippery anyway, and
he seemed as double-jointed as a trained mime. But
when they began to haul him up again to try and support

him between them he seemed to wake, not suddenly, but gradually. It was literally a stiffening process. As if testing out his limbs and muscles, uncertain how exactly they worked, he stood more or less straight, but as if quite, quite giddy. Had they let go of him he would have fallen, with a crash, on his face, and probably would not have remembered quickly enough how to bring an arm up to save himself.

While Ramrod supported him, Tate unfastened, then removed the helmet. The rubber suit had a safety tongue which came over the chin and pulled in his jaw so he looked rabbit-teethed. His complexion was white and wet with sweat as if in a high fever. His eyes were very, very dark and dull. His hair fell over his forehead like a medieval fringe. He was, in other words, practically unrecognizable; an anonymous peasant taken from the rack about to be asked questions in a language which he did not understand. They supported him all the way down the steps to the chair and sat him there in front of the bright light. For some (as yet, unexplained) reason he did not blink. It was as if his ordinary motor reflexes, those reactions by which we instantly protect ourselves, had been so confused that they might as well have been disconnected altogether. He smelt quite revolting. At some time he had evidently vomited and had, of course, sweated profusely.

Norman, according to Ramrod's instructions, came in with some coffee now and put it on the table. He had been told to say nothing, but had he been allowed to speak he could not have found words. Sharpey had looked sick enough, the times when he had been extracted, but he had looked like Sharpey. This man was not Longman.

Ramrod tapped Norman on the arm, bringing him back to his senses, and the boy then went out again, back to Lab B. As Tate in a very friendly way, persuaded Longman to take some coffee, Ramrod returned to the gantry and there retrieved the microphone that had stood by the speaking tube. The connexion was only just long enough to reach the trestle table below.

He had to thread it through the railings by the steps to make the shortest distance. Placing it on the table he said, "Testing, testing," only that.

Tate, meantime, was talking to Longman who had managed a quarter of the mug of coffee and seemed, a little, to thaw out. He blinked and slowly tried to turn his head away from the light.

"Look at me," Tate said, comfortingly. "That's better, isn't it? . . . You recognize me. You're all right. You'll feel fine."

Longman nodded, not as if he recognized Tate but as if he were surprised that these beings from another world could talk.

Norman then opened the door, signalled to Ramrod that the reception was okay. Then he went back to the tapes to control the recording of the interview.

Ramrod took his place in the shadow opposite Longman and nodded to Tate who was still persuading his "friend" to take some coffee.

"You know me, don't you?" he asked again.

At last, Longman answered, and he seemed more surprised than they were, to have found his voice.

"I know you."

"Good —" Tate said, encouragingly, fast on his cue. "And I should jolly well think so, too. . . . I'll be insulted if you've forgotten my name."

Longman was staring at Ramrod, who held his gaze. Now he turned back to Tate. His own personality seemed to return, with a faint smile.

"Of course not. I haven't forgotten."

Loudly, abruptly, and coldly Ramrod asked him, "What is his name?" and Longman looked first afraid, then lost. He seemed to want to move away but be too uncertain of his motor actions to dare try.

Ramrod spoke again, in the same cold tone. "You said you hadn't forgotten it."

Longman stared back at him, then nodded dumbly.

Ramrod pressed. "What is it? Tell me what his name is."

Tate comforted with a smile. "Of course he knows it."

Longman, childishly, desperately, said, "Yes, I do."

"What then?" Ramrod asked icily.

"I . . . I."

"Think! Think! . . . I'll give you five seconds. . . . One, two —"

"I do know it. I do," Longman said again, more desperately, like a frightened schoolboy.

"Then tell me! At once!"

The parallel with Bonvoubois at this point was very close. Longman swayed from side to side in the same bearish way. But Tate came to his rescue. Feigning displeasure, he turned to Ramrod.

"The man's tired, for God's sake. He knows my name's Tate as well as I know his is Longman. You're being quite unreasonable." Then he turned back to Longman who was smiling and nodding again and again, enthusiastically, with pleasure and relief. Tate touched his arm, and asked quietly and sensibly, "What does it feel like? Asleep for a hundred years?"

Longman steadied. Then at last he answered, "No."

"What, then?" Ramrod asked.

Longman did not look back at him, but down at the rough wood of the table as he answered, with a little giggle, "Awake for a hundred years."

Suddenly Ramrod said, with a sigh, "It's perfectly clear from his answers that there's nothing to be gained by cross-examination at this stage."

Longman was trying to say something.

"I want . . . I —"

But Ramrod cut across him. "There's only one course—"

"Oh." Tate frowned, looked back at Longman. "I can't think you're right."

Longman already guessed what was in the air. Terror returned to his eyes.

Ramrod was saying, "Not necessarily for as long again."

"No." Tate differed. "He was at the limit," and at

that point panic broke in again. Longman beat his fist against the shaky trestle table so the lamp nearly fell over, as he screamed:

"I'm not going back in there! I —"

"Of course you aren't," Tate comforted at once.

Longman shook his fist at Ramrod.

"Tell that bastard to get out of here. Get out of my lab, you bloody —" His abuse poured out, obscenely, until Ramrod, pompously, severely, quickly, and loudly cut in:

"You seem to forget your responsibilities, Doctor Longman. We are conducting a controlled experiment. As adviser to that experiment I believe it would be wiser to put you back in the tank for a further period."

Longman turned frantically to Tate. The abuse had gone. He was afraid and hysterical. "No, no . . . don't let him do that. I'll kill myself. I'll —"

Tate reassured him. "Quietly, quietly - quiet. I promise." He turned back to Ramrod. "We can't risk it. Truly we can't. Apart from anything else he has four children who rely on him."

"Yes, I've four children —" Longman echoed, pathetically.

There followed, then, the crux of the interrogation. Both Ramrod and Tate were fairly tense, observing Longman very closely. Longman's expression was curiously ambivalent. He was both afraid, so it seemed, and trusting, aware that with Tate, in these circumstances there was really no reason to be afraid. It was as if he could not help himself; as if he were aware that his two examiners were subtly but systematically undermining his belief and love for Oonagh, but still could do nothing to stop them.

"How many children?" Ramrod asked.

"Four," Longman said, more carefully.

"I thought there was a wife," Ramrod said to Tate, and got the reply:

"There is . . . but —"

"Surely to God she can manage the children?"

Tate hesitated. He played his part with great skill.

He glanced at Longman then leant back to speak to Ramrod. He spoke privately yet audibly.

"There *is* a wife. But she's not much of a help, you know? Quite immature, jealous of her own children, but that isn't the real point . . ." He turned back to Longman who seemed to hear but not fully understand, at this point. He said, "It isn't quite the point, is it?"

Longman seemed quite mystified. Tate squeezed his arm again in a friendly way.

"Is it?"

"No, no," Longman said quite puzzled, yet sure that he should keep close to Tate.

Ramrod said, "From the information that I have been given the opposite would seem to be true. Mrs. Longman is talked of as a most sympathetic woman."

"Sympathetic?"

"Sympathetic - competent, anyway."

"Oh, she's competent. She cooks marvellously, doesn't she, Longman?"

"Yes."

"Rice dishes - pilaffs especially?"

"Oh, yes."

"And stews?"

"Yes."

"But competence —" Tate smiled sadly. "Well . . . A man needs more than that."

Almost by reflex now, Longman nodded to everything Tate said. Ramrod spoke again.

"If you're referring to her sexual attractions —"

"I am."

"But here again," Ramrod said swiftly, "My information is that the couple are particularly, even peculiarly fond —"

"Peculiarly," Tate said flatly, "is about right."

"What's that supposed to mean?"

"Those picnics we've all heard about - the forty nights and forty days. . . . Well —" He winked at Longman, who nodded.

Ramrod said, "I must ask you not to indulge in a private conversation at this point."

"It isn't easy."

"Not easy," Longman, dimly, agreed.

"Even if it isn't easy, let's get it clear. Are you suggesting that there's something unnatural in his relationship with his wife?"

"Unnatural isn't the right word. Is it, Longman?"

"Good God, no." Longman seemed rather drunk now: a yes-man with too much beer on board.

Tate said, "If you must have it frankly, the whole thing's a bluff. Let's leave it at that."

"How, bluff?"

"Well, for heaven's sake —" Tate seemed fed up with Ramrod now. He raised his eyebrows to Longman and whispered, "The plodding, military mind . . ."

"We must have this clearly stated."

"He doesn't find her attractive," Tate said loudly. "But this is a very private thing. And quite irrelevant, so let's leave it there."

"I don't find it irrelevant."

"For God's sake," Tate said angrily. "Why should we tell you our personal secrets? I've no intention of telling you mine. Longman does marvels with a woman he doesn't love —"

"Love—" Ramrod echoed, disparagingly. "Meaning what?"

"Please—"

"Meaning what?"

Angrily, again, for Longman, Tate answered loud and fast. "He doesn't want to sleep with her, all right?"

"Why not?"

"Because he doesn't love her. He doesn't like her smell, her taste, the sight of her body - whatever it is makes up sexual attraction. . . . I'm sure you can tell us, Major. You must be familiar with the Shepherd Market *salons*?"

Longman laughed at that.

"Is this true, Longman?" Ramrod asked, and again Longman seemed bewildered. Ramrod asked again: "Is it true?"

Tate said, "You might as well admit it. Honestly. He'll go on and on."

"True," Longman said. Then he seemed utterly confused. They both sat silently watching him as he rose to his feet, determined, it seemed, to say something with great force.

"You - you —"

But his eyes suddenly turned up. The effort of standing was too much for him. The room must have swung up and round and round. With a heavy crash he fell half across the table, half across Tate, in a dead faint.

Tate shouted at the top of his voice, desperately. "Norman! Norman, for Christ's sake, an ambulance! Ring an ambulance." Then letting Longman's head down gently on to the cork floor he looked up at Ramrod, and he said in a low voice. "What have you made me do?"

It comes twice on the tape, before Norman switched off. Louder, the second time, Tate's voice filled with horror and fear:

"Major, what have you made me do?"

15

Calder was as angry as a nanny whose ward has narrowly escaped death. Fussily, he shouted, "Move away, will you, all of you? You can't help here. . . ." But students are trained to be curious. Calder almost stamped his foot. "For heaven's sake, you're educated people, aren't you? Not inquisitive children. . . ."

At this, they moved back a little, but not too far away

from the commotion at the door of the little hut called
Isolation. A moment before, two ambulance men had
carried out a stretcher, on which Longman lay, well
tucked round with blankets. He was pale and corpse-like,
his eyes closed, his nose to the sky. It was beginning
to grow dark and the martins and swallows were dashing
about between the buildings. Most of the labs were empty
or the crowd might have been larger. But there were
enough there to produce that certain ripple of noise,
as they were all surprised. Longman had woken up.

Norman at once knelt beside him, on the grass, and
the students had to move a little to try and see him.
Norman called anxiously back, "He's coming round,"
and Calder moved across.

Calder said, "We shan't take any risks," with hollow
ministerial authority, then to Longman, who was trying
to sit up, he said, "My dear man, you must lie down.
Please lie down."

Longman's answer was loud and clear and it delighted
the students who had come closer again.

"Lie down? Why the hell should I?" he asked. Then
sitting bolt upright he continued, "What's going on?"
He waved a bare arm towards the students. He shouted,
"Norman, tell these vultures to clear off."

But it was Calder who took up that request. He
harangued them again. "Look here, I don't know which
faculty you belong to, or which college, but we could
do without your encouragement. Please be so good as
to get out of here, at once —"

One of the students said, easily, "Can you tell us
what happened?"

"No, I cannot —"

"Has he been in the tank?"

"Get out. Go away, d'you hear? Go away!"

As he shooed them off Norman talked quietly and
kindly to Longman.

"I've been really worried, doctor. Thank God you
—"

"I can't think why," Longman said, in the same bright,
loud voice. "I've never felt better. But there's a great

deal around here that seems to call for explanation."

Calder circled back. "Longman, you've been unconscious for some time."

"I'm not now." He looked angrily at the stretcher. "Help me off this damned thing —" But as he moved, whipping off the blanket, he realized for the first time that he was quite naked, and pulled back the blanket, swiftly. "Good God . . . Norman?"

"Yes, doctor?"

"For Christ's sake get them to haul me back in there —"

"You're bound for the Radcliffe Infirmary —"

"Get them to take me back, I say. . . . Come on, pall-bearers," he shouted at the two uncertain ambulance men. "Get me back, will you? And don't hang about or I'll catch cold."

They looked at Calder. He was speaking to Tate and Ramrod who had now arrived at the door of the lab. Longman shouted so loudly that his voice rang round the nearby buildings. "Tatty, kindly kick these men until they lift me back whence I came."

Calder signalled to the ambulance men, and they picked him up and took him back to the lab. At the door Calder must have said something soothing or cautionary to Longman. It did not go down well. Again the voice rattled against all the modern labs around, echoing from glass to concrete.

"So would you be bloody angry if you woke up bollock-naked in the quad."

Everybody always said it. Calder could be too easily underestimated, as a caricature of himself, a fussy man without talent, meddling in laboratory, college, and even city affairs; the committee man, *par excellence*. He was not so silly. He did have a talent, which was simply that he recognized the talent, and in Sharpey's case, the genius of others. He knew very well what the bright boys thought of him, but he also knew - as Sharpey had recognized - that there were many things which he could do better than the rest of them put together. He therefore

believed firmly that he would make a better permanent
director of the labs than anybody else. There are men
like him in every lab, in every department, in every branch
of the civil service, and in every industry. They are never
recognized until they are dead, when suddenly half
a dozen top men admit that the Calder in the case gave
them their first job, or put them into such-and-such a
field of research, or even organized the mortgage on
their house. Then, many years later, when the new Calder
has taken the place of authority, everybody says, "The
difference between this man and Calder, is that this
one is out purely for self glorification. Old Calder, one
must admit, had the good of the lab, and the college,
and the university, and the city, at heart."

Norman's reading of Calder's character, as presented
to Ramrod, proved only the narrowness of Norman's
vision. And all of them, now - Tate, Norman, even
Ramrod - were guilty of misinterpreting Calder's motives.
They thought he had been frightened for one reason, namely that if an accident had occurred at this stage then that
would put paid to his chances of the permanent appoint-
ment as Professor and Director of the labs.

Calder was better than that. He dearly wished to
be professor not only because he had worked for it,
but because he wanted to be part of the history of a
lab in which fine research had already been performed,
and which, he believed, had a huge and important future.
In this sense, therefore, his indignation was not so ridiculous. He paced up and down Lab A, preparing his
attack as Longman got dressed.

Meantime, Tate checked Longman's pulse and Longman
asked, "Okay?"

"Normal," Tate said, looking at him very steadily.
Neither he nor Ramrod ever took their eyes off him,
searching for some clue.

Longman seemed to refuse their inquisitive looks,
determined to take life, at this point, at the first level;
to play it with shrugs and jokes about nudes in the quad.
He was restless, almost energetic, moving about the
lab as he put on his jacket and tie.

"Sound as a bell," he said. "I'd be surprised if I wasn't. I feel very good."

"I'm glad to hear it," Calder replied, "even if I am more than surprised."

Longman went over to the steps up to the tank and held on to them for a moment, then Calder decided to make his little speech.

"I have rung your wife," he said, "and I mean to have a long talk with her."

Tate and Ramrod exchanged glances. They had told Calder nothing of the interrogation. But it turned out to be a coincidental reference. Calder went on, "I shall tell her you are to go away now for a long holiday, and a restful one."

Longman grinned. "I've just finished a six weeks' holiday."

"I don't think so," Calder said. "I don't think that's quite true. I'm not as stupid as I look, Longman. . . . I know the sort of strains this kind of work must have put on you. And I'm taking no risks. Fishing, travelling, anything that suits you, which you can afford, but it is essential you have complete relaxation."

"I feel very good. I told you."

"And I told you, I'm glad, but I'm not convinced. . . . I want you to know I'm quite shocked by what you've been doing here. . . . Eight hours . . . . Eight hours in that diabolical bath and not so much as a 'by your leave'. You realize I would be held responsible? I'm shocked. . . . The immaturity of such an impulsive course. . . . This is a place for scientists, you know, not heroic schoolboys. . . . And you, Major. You, too, you shock me. No man should have been subjected to Isolation for that length of time. . . . Longman, you'll have a complete rest."

Tate seemed restive. "There are some ends to be tied up on today's work. . . ."

Calder shouted "No" and Ramrod gave Tate a sign to say, "Don't argue with him, now," meaning clearly that he would endeavour to persuade him later. Calder said, "I don't want any protests or whisperings. . . .

Major, you should understand an order when it is given. I am director of these labs. I am responsible for the work that is done here. I have taken a decision, and it's irreversible. I'll be talking to Mrs. Longman as well."

There was a little silence. Calder's seriousness was for a moment respected. He said, quietly then, "Thank God, you seem to be in one piece," to Longman, touched him on the arm in an awkward way, but not unaffectionately, then, not without dignity, wished them good night.

"Good morning," Longman said, as if correcting him, and Calder turned at the door. He looked at his watch. "I make it nine p.m."

Longman was not joking. "I don't believe you," he said.

Tate checked. "He's perfectly right."

Calder said, "It's two minutes past, to be exact," then wishing them good night again, he left.

There was a pause, then over by the steps, Longman began to laugh and laugh. Their anxious faces only made him laugh more.

He said, "It's really terrible. It's an unbearable anti-climax. It's the mountain bringing forth the mouse."

They looked at him, bewildered. He went on:

"I could swear it was breakfast time tomorrow and it's only supper time today. We go through the whole cabaret, the kicking and the screaming, and all I feel due for is coffee and ham and eggs!" He sat down on the steps and laughed again, aware that they were staring at him. He hardly bothered to glance up when he said, "You look like a couple of burglars," and it was an accurate description.

There was nothing hysterical, however, about this laughter. There was perhaps a note of relief, but on the whole he seemed simply bowled over by the oldest joke of the lot - man's absurdity. Yet this is not the whole truth. An accurate description of Longman at this time is necessary. There was a certain ambivalence, a mischie-vousness, so subtle that it is almost indefinable. He seemed to be saying, "Don't think I don't notice you watching me. Don't think I don't know why. Yet don't think that I am going to admit that I see you looking at me oddly." It was a curious, youthful, almost flirtatious quality as if he were playing with them, and the more solemn they became, the happier he seemed to be.

Tate at last broached the subject. "Obviously we would prefer to keep you under observation for a while."

"Why, Tatty?"

"I think it would be wise. A simple precaution."

"Precaution against what, Major? How am I supposed to behave?"

The two burglars hesitated, in confusion, and Longman laughed again.

"No. . . . You poor idiots. . . . You do not need to take precautions. Relax. Be gay with me. I'm a man snatched from the gallows. The period of observation would be a period of time wasted."

Still the others looked unhappy, then quite suddenly, factually, Longman said:

"I'm not pulling your legs - well, perhaps a little, but I'll stop doing so now. I know what you said. I remember it. Tate, whispering, and that SS man there. I remember it all, children. Don't look so glum . . . And what a clever idea. . . . That's our Major, or did Tatty think it up —"

Tate answered, too strongly, "No, I swear. . . . I was worried. . . . D'you mean you really remember?"

"Tatty's always worried," Longman said, rather seriously, and the way he looked seemed to indicate that he might say something cruel. Evidently he changed his mind. He let him off lightly. "There is no need to be. Your experiment didn't work. The tank is not such an ogre as we thought. . . ."

They would not, could not have accepted all this at its face value, much as both wanted to, for Calder's words on responsibility had made even Ramrod pause to reflect. But they were then to be relieved in the most dramatic and joyful way. Oonagh came into the lab. Calder had told her where to come, and hurrying, almost breathlessly, she arrived in their midst, stopped equally suddenly. Then she looked, with fear, at her husband.

He stretched out his hands and said, "Poor old Otter."

Oonagh stopped herself running to his arms. Perhaps the room itself restrained her. She stood where she was, pausing for a second as if she were thanking God. Then rather seriously, still standing her ground, she said, "Calder tells me you want breakfast."

"Correct!" Longman said.

"You're all right?"

Longman grinned. "I'm even clean behind the ears."

She said, "I was so desperately worried. They rang me." Oonagh's eyes looked very much darker than usual. She never took them off her husband. When she spoke seriously she always spoke neatly, finishing her sentences, almost in a literary fashion.

"As I lifted the receiver I was certain there was bad news."

Ramrod said, "I think we can assure you there's none."

Longman was watching his wife with that same ambivalent, cheerful light in his eye. She did not respond to it. She spoke solemnly again.

"About five minutes before they rang I had a horrible premonition."

"Hush," Longman said. "Later. . . . We're all right, my dear. We're whole. You need only take me from here and cook me my large late evening breakfast."

Longman turned to Tate. "May I go, Doctor?"

Tate could hardly believe his luck. His shoulders dropped an inch as he smiled and said, "No further questions."

"Major?"

"Enjoy your ham and eggs. You'd better come for a physical check in the morning, but for the rest, dismiss."

When the couple had gone, Tate and Ramrod wearily collected their coats, leaving Norman to clear the tapes and empty the tank. Then the two men wandered out of the lab. The Lagonda had already disappeared. They took deep gulps of fresh air.

" 'Suddenly everybody burst out singing,' " Ramrod

said with the platitudinous gratitude of a simple soldier, and pulled back his shoulders. "Not breakfast for me. A big gin."

Tate said, "Celebration?"

Ramrod nodded. "Certainly," he answered, seriously. "For an experiment like this to have failed makes the day an unqualified success. I shall have to be careful not to get drunk tonight. I'm told I behave in an embarrassingly kittenish manner under the influence."

Tate said, "I'm not sure it's absolutely unqualified. We rather forget Longman's object. He seems to have forgotten it himself, seeing Oonagh again, but we should be thankful for that." ·

"You mean Sharpey?"

"I do mean Sharpey."

Ramrod sniffed. "Between you and me," he said, "there's no surprise there, Tate. He'd been building to this all his life. I'll be frank with you. If it were only to clear a dead man's name I wouldn't have let Longman go through today's ordeal. Indeed I believe the success may be greater than we know. It sounds to me as if her majesty's enemies have paid good money for nothing." He laughed suddenly and heartily at that. "And there's an excuse for a second big gin."

16

"You are tired, I think. Lean down to the dashboard and I'll see more. . . . I believe Calder's right for once. We'll go fishing, in some deserted island."

"Where the skies are cloudy all day."

Oonagh paused. Then she said, "You look younger, I think," but he did not bother to answer her.

The Lagonda was parked this evening where it had been parked almost every evening for the past forty-eight days, but they had come too late. The sun had already set, and there were owls, not nightingales. The beginning of a breeze turned the tips of the poplar trees in a sad bow, and the moon was dimmed by clouds. The river, behind them, was not silvery, but dark like treacle and there were eyes in the yew hedges; torture, it seemed, in the contorted limbs of big elm trees.

"Love me?" Oonagh hugged his arm, and he sat stock still, to answer:

"You know I do."

"I'm cold," she said, then tried again to pull him a little closer.

"Perhaps we'd better go back," he said, perfectly kindly. "You mustn't catch cold."

"Longman, I've got something to tell you." His head did not turn. She could see only the side of his face by the light from the dashboard and he looked severe.

"What sort of thing?" he asked.

"You're very dim, really, Longman. You're blind and austere and nice: my absent-minded lover." Her words seemed to get lost in the hedges and thicker trees that followed the canal, to the south of them; the canal that led past the patch where the foxes play. She said, "I'm pregnant," and might as well have said it to the wind.

At last he asked, with a tired smile, "Is that bad?"

"No, darling," she said, trying to cover her disappointment. Then she gathered again. "I'm glad. Don't smile so faintly. Smile widely because it's not a joke. It's serious and I'm glad, love, so glad. It's a deep bell tolling, that's how serious it is, this baby."

"Extraordinary girl you are to drive ten miles to tell me."

She frowned. For the first time a note of something graver than passing anxiety stole into her voice. She spoke very flatly.

"But don't you see why I wanted to come here? For heaven's sake, didn't we drive here the day it all started."

"I remember," he answered coldly, and again there was a long pause. She was not touching him now. She saw the back of his hand, resting on the seat beside her but did not reach out to it. She did not quite dare, she did not know why. She was like a wife who does not want to show her husband how sure she is of his infidelity. That would be to crack her own last chance of healing love.

She said quickly, "Perhaps it isn't such a good place after all," and a tree creaked in the wind.

She said, "I wish we hadn't come here now. That deep bell rang another note." He shrugged and smiled at her again, the same smile with much breadth but no depth at all.

"You're getting all weird and gaelic," he said.

"Love me, Longman," she replied very desperately. "Just now, a cold hand came right inside and clutched."

He did not kiss her as he smiled again and said, with patience, it seemed:

"Love you very much!" He reached forward, instead, and turned the ignition key.

She said, "I wish I had a coat," because if she had, she would have buttoned it round her tightly, to feel safer, miles from anywhere, beside a stranger.

PART THREE

17

If there is one moral animal on earth it is a woman in love. Once she has fallen she is unswerving. The pain she will endure and the humiliations she will suffer in the cause of her single love are beyond males' comprehension, if not beyond his boast. So it was with Oonagh.

Tate promised to visit the Longmans regularly after the experiment, but he did not find it easy to do so. He never knew whether Longman had told Oonagh the details of the experiment, and especially the interrogation, and for reasons he understood too well, but refused to face, he did not want to speak to her of his own part in the proceedings. It was therefore a great relief to him, when only a week after Ramrod's departure, the Longmans, children, Lagonda, and all, packed off to the Continent for their extended holiday.

It was two weeks into the winter term, which is to say early in November (in fact, on the afternoon of Guy Fawkes day), when Tate saw them all again. He had a reason for calling, and a pleasant one, but after he spoke with the children, by the front gate, he wished strongly that he had not come. It was a gloomy enough afternoon with those blue grey clouds which make us feel forsaken.

"How's the raft?" Tate asked, and they scowled and pushed the toes of their shoes through the gravel. "How's the *Kon Tiki?*"

"Oh, that," Penny said wearily. "That's all washed up. We've been around since then, if you really want to know."

Paul said, "For months."

"We've been to seven countries. Italy, France —"

Tate was looking at the house. It reminded him of Sharpey's death. He asked, "Is Longman in?" and they all turned away from him. "Well, is he?"

"He's always in," Paul said, as they wandered away, then Tate was on his own. The front door was closed, and knowing the Longman household, Tate pushed the bell without confidence. To his surprise, it rang.

After a moment, Oonagh came to the door. She was by now seven months pregnant and she did not look her usual self. She was considerably thinner, her face almost haggard, tired, and strained. Her hair was straggly, her eyes hollowed. Tate did his best to disguise the sense of shock he felt at seeing her like this. She did not seem interested in his reaction, either way.

Very flatly she said, "Tate . . . A message from Calder, I suppose?"

Tate said gently, "No."

Reluctantly, she opened the door a little wider. "You'd better come in."

In silence he followed her, but she did not stop in the hall which was looking very tidy and ship-shape. The children's invasion had evidently been repelled. Oonagh behaved curiously. She did not pause but walked straight over to the staircase, saying, in the most off-hand manner.

"Longman's in there." She indicated the downstairs sitting room, but evidently she did not want to show him in herself. She was already a few steps up the stairs when Tate found his voice.

"Look, it's not an official visit - Is something wrong?"

She stared at him. Heaven knows what she bit back before she said, flatly again, "Nothing."

"Aren't you coming in?"

Before she could answer, the door behind Tate opened and Longman appeared. Oonagh raised her eyes to him. In a voice that was jeering, not joking, he said:

"Answer the gentleman."

Tate turned back to greet him and as he did so, saying, "Hallo," Oonagh started upstairs, swiftly.

But Longman called her back. "Oonagh?" She stopped, obediently, with her head lowered, but she did not turn back. Longman moved forward to the bottom of the stairs, but he addressed Tate, not his wife, as he said, rather lazily:

"Isn't it amazing what pregnancy does to a woman? She's always shuffling up and down those stairs. Some eat clay-pipes, others drink ginger beer. She shuffles up and down stairs . . . How d'you think she looks?"

Tate was frightened. "Very well," he said weakly.

Longman called to Oonagh who was still frozen, half way upstairs.

"D'you hear that? You're being complimented by the ex-lodger. Turn about . . ." She stood stock still. Louder, he said, "Turn about!" and when she obeyed he smiled a fat smile. "There," he said. "Come down, step by step with due care. All the way."

Again, step by step, slowly, she obeyed. Longman went on, "We won't eat you. . . ." Then he turned suddenly to Tate and said, "D'you remember I used to call her 'Otter' sometimes, in the old days, in the days of *amour, amour, amour*?" He laughed at such an outlandish memory. She had none of the otter's charm now.

Oonagh then asked Tate, very quietly, "Would you like some coffee?"

"No thanks . . . I haven't really time. I only came to —" Longman intercepted. "To tell me I was bloody lazy and I ought to do some teaching? So right you are. I wonder why I don't. It isn't exactly a garden of roses here. But I've been busy reorganizing a household which our pregnant Bohemian friend there had - not to put too strong a point on it - let slip." He cast her a glance of utter hatred which made Tate clench his fists. It did not seem to affect Oonagh. It was as if she were beyond expecting anything else. Lightly again, Longman said to her, "Tate really thinks you're looking well."

Tate shifted, then tried to ease things. He smiled and said, "I haven't seen you since you came back —" Then he broke off. He could not continue to smile in front of Oonagh. She looked as if she had not slept for days, so resigned and exhausted had she become. Tate slapped the bannister with the palm of his hand. "I sent you an invitation to a party."

Longman frowned. Acting so broadly that the lie was obvious, he then pretended he had never heard tell of the party.

"No?"

"RSVP," Tate said.

Longman switched back to Oonagh.

"But, my dear?"

"I showed it to you," she said quietly.

Again Longman acted broadly, with a wide gesture, pretending to disbelieve her.

"Oh, honey —"

"I'm sorry, Tate," she said neatly, with more feeling, as if her control would go.

"God!" Longman shouted. "God, but you're so dishonest. All women aren't dishonest, are they, Tate?"

Tate turned away. He mumbled, "It's tonight anyway. If you didn't notice it, this is Guy Fawkes night. . . . Are you coming?" He looked at Oonagh as he asked, but got no reaction. She turned sadly to Longman.

Longman shrugged. "You've got a tongue, haven't you?"

She blinked. She was still standing one or two steps from the bottom of the stairs. She said, "Honestly, Tate, I don't feel terribly like a party." She looked down at her body. She said, simply, "All this —"

"I see." Tate was not surprised. But again he hesitated

to leave. "Anyway, it's on the barge. Mine and my next door neighbour's. You must meet Annabelle. That's her name. She's quite a girl."

"Let's," Longman said.

"Anyway," Tate said again, unhappily, "plenty to drink, if you change your minds."

"I shan't change mine," Longman replied, heartily. "Not a chance of it. I'm most certainly coming. What time does the whistle blow?"

Tate looked back at Oonagh again. Oonagh looked at the ground.

"Starts at eight," Tate said, then moved towards the front door. "I've still got loads of drink to buy."

"Buy away, my friend. . . . Oonagh?"

"Yes." She looked afraid.

"Show the gentleman to the door."

She nodded, and he added in the most horrible way - "Otter." As she blinked at that, wounded again by it, he protested. "But it's a term of endearment —" She walked across to the door while Tate protested he could manage; not to bother. Longman stood in the middle of the hall. Still smiling he said, "Show him to the garden gate, if you like. Tell him all about it." Then his smile went. With a real, waspish sting, he said, "Whisper in his ear - yatterty - yatterty - yat!" then disappeared back into the sitting room.

On the doorstep, Tate turned, racked with anxiety.

"Oonagh —"

But she was not prepared to talk. Not a word. Swiftly, but not rudely she pushed the door shut, saying only, "Bye-bye."

She returned, with small steps across the hall and then hurried upstairs. Outside, in a blue world, Tate turned and wandered away.

18

Soon after Ramrod left Staff College at Camberly he opened a brothel in Verona, an occasion which he remembered with both pleasure and pride. The brothel had been organized by Americans for Americans, and it boasted fifteen more or less Italian girls but the Madame, as so frequently in these cases, was a Dundee-French lady. So formidable was her charm and strict her sense of etiquette that the American officers gathered there for the opening night grew shy, unhappy, and unsexy. The general commanding therefore invited Ramrod, a guest with their Headquarters' contingent, to do the right thing. Ramrod did so, upstairs, with energy and elegance. Afterwards he came to the top of the stairs and waving a frilly handkerchief, declared the place well and truly consummated. He remembered the day only when he was feeling satisfied with things, and approaching Oxford, at eight o'clock that Guy Fawkes evening, he had no worries. He was all dressed up for a party, wholly prepared to drink himself kittenish, game for any opening ceremony which might present itself.

He could not even be put off by the Oxford taxi-man's gentle contrariness which had infuriated inhabitants and visitors for thirty years. Ramrod raised his hat, uncertain whether anyone with such a grand Churchillian face could be a cabbie.

"Are you free?"

"No, sir," was the taxi-man's reply, because "no, sir" was his first reply to every request. Those who knew

Aubrey, however, would not have been surprised at his subsequent action. He reached back and opened the door for Ramrod, saying, "In you get, sir." Aubrey was like a man whose face had got stuck when the wind changed. It was as if he had joked, facetiously, too often, and now was stuck with it. Bored by his own sense of humour he still played his role as Contrary.

Ramrod read from Tate's invitation card. He explained, "It's a barge - about a mile down from Folly Bridge. D'you know where that is?"

"Never heard of it," Aubrey said, and started his terrible old car. Ramrod leant back with a sigh, and a smile. He meant to enjoy himself. He did not know what lay in store for him.

Fireworks were exploding all round Gloucester Green and there were some bonfires in various college gardens. But Aubrey had not bargained on the crowd in the Turl, a narrow enough street at the best of times.

It was a mass of undergraduates, on the whole, good-tempered, but searching for something on which to expend their excess energies. At this point they seemed to have set on an Indian Restaurant, which had wisely barred its doors. The whole crowd was chanting, "Free Curry at the Taj, we want free curry —," when Aubrey swung into the street, blew his horn, then braked hard. The students were delighted to find a new point of interest. Up went a roar of appreciation, as they moved in on the old car.

Aubrey was nothing if not stoical. "Here we go, sir," he said to Ramrod, flatly and unworriedly. A couple of dozen boys, meantime, had surrounded the taxi and with a "one, two, three," they lifted it clear off the ground, then let it drop with a bump that nearly winded Ramrod. But Staff College at Camberly and subsequent brothel-opening experiences had taught Ramrod to smile during and throughout all civil disorders.

"Pay no attention, sir," Aubrey said.

They began then to rock the car from side to side, trying to make Ramrod sea-sick, but it only made him giggle. At last they tired of it and Aubrey, very politely, addressed the ring-leader.

"Quite finished, are we, sir?"

There were cheers and cries of "Let him go." With great dignity Aubrey replied, "Thank you very much, sir," then driving through the rest of the mob, with one hand on the horn, he spoke less charitably. The beatic smile belied his mutterings.

"Little pimples, so they are. Educated stupid. They're not what they used to be. Oh, no. . . . Bloody lucky, lucky Jims."

Ramrod had to leave the taxi at the edge of the damp meadow and walk the last half mile to the barges which Aubrey indicated. There was a notice at this point, reading "Tate's Pad", and some huge bonfires burnt on the towpath outside two dilapidated old barges which looked as if they still carried coal. On these lived Tate and his next door neighbour, one Annabelle.

Annabelle, in Oxford, needs no introduction. There have always been Annabelles and there always will be, until the proctors turn to pillars of salt. She was merely the most eccentric contemporary representative of a long, long line of Annabelles. A gentleman's education, it could be said, was not complete without her: Eton, Oxford, and Annabelle. She was a battered thirty-one year-old with a manner so exaggerated as to make Fenella Fielding sound like plain Jane, but beneath the bruises and the erratic dialogue there beat, she said herself, a heart of pure gold slush.

Ramrod said, "How d'you do," to her as he stepped on to Tate's barge, without having any idea who she might be. Evidently taking him to be a student she said merely, "Christ, they're getting younger every term," but then Norman approached with a drink.

"Hallo, Major?"

"Norman," Ramrod said with pleasure. But he had a flat, flat foot, our man. He asked, "You helping out?"

Norman checked. "I'm a guest."

"I'm sorry, Norman. I didn't mean —"

"You did," Norman replied. "So drink your drink and forget it."

Ramrod had the grace to blush, then Norman asked him:

"You're not here officially, are you?"

"No, no . . ." Ramrod assured him. "Purely for the jokes. . . . Where's my host, d'you suppose?"

"Tate? He's inside somewhere. Try, it's dead uncomfortable," he added, meaning the cabin of the barge.

Ramrod found it difficult to move up the deck of the barge which was thick with people, dancing and talking; students, dons, and hangers-on. He retired, deciding to walk up-shore and step on to the barge again by the plank leading to the well. As he did so, however, he noticed that his hostess had moved away from her place by the second gang-plank. She was on the deck of her own barge, only a yard or two away, and Ramrod suddenly realized that she was not alone. She was being kissed very hard. He would have moved on, had he not heard the man's voice. It was Longman's.

"Pirate's proposal," he was saying, a little drunkenly. "Your choice, lady. Say 'yes' or I'll shove you over."

Annabelle shook her head and looked at her latest conquest carefully. She commented on the subtlety of man. But Longman interrupted her. Holding his glass high, in what, for some reason, he seemed to imagine to be a pious gesture, he said:

"With this glass, I thee wed."

"Oh, no, dear," Annabelle at once replied. "That one makes me cry. It's got such a nasty end."

Longman shrugged.

"Shall we try a burial at sea?"

She nodded like a jolly little doll. "Oh, yes, that would be much nicer," she said. "More cheerful - you know?"

Longman again pulled her to him and kissed her and she kicked up a leg behind her. Not promptly, but at last she pulled away. Longman was drunker than had at first appeared. Like a big boy blind at a Rodeo he said, "It's a party, isn't it?"

Annabelle was shaking her head, looking up at him. In her funny, croaky, neat little voice, she said, "I'm mad, I'm mad at you."

"What did I do?"

"I've been waiting all week for you."

Longman frowned at this; turned up the palm of his hand.

"We never met before."

"That's why I'm mad, dear," she answered, and led the way round to the well of the second barge.

Ramrod followed, at a tactful distance, persuading himself that he did so on account of anxiety over the couple's safety.

Barge parties are sometimes famous for the hats, but usually for the drownings. The couple passed a curious wide skylight through which they could see the cabin lit up below, and Annabelle, glancing down suddenly, now stopped, stepping back into the shadow.

"Sh!" she said. "Another couple."

Longman peered forward, nodded in agreement, then peered forward again.

He said, "That's no couple, that's my wife." Annabelle was not so insensitive. She knew a lot about men's moods. Uncertainly but kindly, and incidentally quite unnecessarily she tried to cover the situation.

"It's just a party, isn't it?"

"That's no party, that's my wife —" Longman moved forward, to look again. Then he turned back to Annabelle.

"That's my wife, that was."

"Oh, don't be silly —"

Longman at last understood what Annabelle feared. He crossed his fingers to indicate crossed-wires, a conversation that had gone hay-wire at a party, as conversations tend to do. Then very lengthily he explained that Oonagh's presence in the cabin below with this other man, Tate, neither surprised him nor hurt him in any way.

"If you want to know," he said, "I can't stomach her," and he shuddered at the thought of her skin.

Annabelle was shocked. She screwed up her face and

said, "No," meaning, "No, don't take any joke that far."

Longman suddenly took action. He flung his glass into the middle of the river, with a fine gesture at Tate's expense, grabbed Annabelle and headed, unsteadily, for the shore.

Ramrod stepped forward to say, "Good evening."

Longman recognized him immediately, but did not stop.

"Eyes right," he shouted. "Eyes left," and dragging Annabelle along he headed up to the tow-path to a point where there were one or two cars, left by drivers who had had enough confidence in their tyres and springs to drive off the road this far. The Lagonda was there.

Ramrod was not so slow as Tate. He had no reason to refuse the truth. Indeed he grabbed at it, and he moved straight away, on to the second barge. As he passed the sky-light window he glanced down and saw Tate walking up and down anxiously. Oonagh was sitting on a curious, specially fitted folding bed, with her hands covering her face.

Ramrod hurried round to the cabin entrance, then paused there for a second, to ask himself if he were not perhaps jumping too fast to false conclusions. He heard Tate say, quietly and nervously:

"Don't cry. Really don't. It's just booze. Just that."

"Cry?" It seemed that she was laughing not crying, and Tate sounded more not less disturbed.

He said, "It's just a bloody Oxford party. You know all my parties go wrong. Annabelle's a fair enough girl. She's solid. She won't —"

"D'you think it's Annabelle that worries me?" Oonagh answered, then added, "Oh, Tate."

She was laughing again when Ramrod stepped down and bending his head came into the little cabin. Tate was taken very much by surprise.

"Hallo, Major, I . . . You've got a drink?"

But Ramrod did not answer that. He was looking with horrified surprise at the face of the woman opposite.

He certainly would never have recognized her. He did not beat about the bush.

"How long has this been going on for?"

Tate prevaricated.

"You're being looked after? . . . I . . . Enjoying yourself, I hope?"

Ramrod did not take his eyes from the girl, who was serious now.

He answered Tate. "I wish I could say I was. I've only just arrived, but I've already seen more than I bargained for."

Oonagh, in a crisp, level voice, said, "Oh, just a party, Major. Just the booze. Just one of those nights. Tate will tell you. Just one of those things."

Ramrod stuck relentlessly to the point.

"Since when has Longman behaved like this?"

Tate said, "Not now, Major, please —"

But Oonagh was prepared to answer. Ramrod's directness impressed her.

Again very levelly, she said, "If you want to know, since the night when he asked for breakfast, six months ago . . . while you all happily vanished."

Ramrod raised a hand to stem another interruption from Tate. He sat down opposite and close to Oonagh. He said calmly, "I don't know how much you've heard about the Isolation experiment." He watched her very carefully.

Tate protested then. "It was clear that the experiment didn't work —"

"Tate, please!" Ramrod said, and at last the full meaning of his deadly seriousness dawned on Oonagh. She looked from one to the other, then said:

"You two did something to him."

"It didn't work," Tate argued.

"Yes, we did," Ramrod admitted firmly. "We did so, responsibly, and it was your husband who first insisted on undergoing the experiment."

"You twisted him. Somewhere you —"

Ramrod stretched out a hand to stop her, as if to

say "All will be explained." But as he did so he could
not prevent himself asking angrily of Tate, "Why the
hell haven't you been in touch with me?"

"Oh, don't blame him," Oonagh said. "Not on that
account anyway. . . . He came round once or twice,
before we went away, but, Major, I've been very British.
Right up to this juncture I've been very stiff upper lip
indeed. . . . Just your sort of girl," she added bitterly.
"British when he started on me about all the little things
that only indicated one thing, namely that there was
everything between us, except love. Then on our holiday,
the fishing in the Pyrenees wasn't a success. I evidently
got in the way. So we decided on Calder's alternative,
travelling. It was more than needling now. Love had
changed into something much more positive than 'no
love'." She sat back and laughed again, and shook her
head. "You really should have been there," she said.
"We've had a ghastly scene in every Capital in Europe."

Tate was all for stopping her. But Ramrod worked
on evidence. He continued to stick ruthlessly to the
point.

"Can you give us an example? It's important."

"I can give you a hundred," she replied. "Malaga,
Madrid," she seemed to go through the scenes in her
mind as she spoke dread names. "Perpignan, worse
in Fontainebleu, but Amsterdam —"

"One example, Mrs. Longman!"

She had already chosen Amsterdam. Her small clenched
fist came up to the bridge of her nose and she leant
forward then, pressing her head hard against her closed
knuckles. It was clear to them both that she would not
get through the story without crying, but they did not
stop her. It was as if she had made up her mind that
the goal had been reached. Here, now for the first
time, she could break down. Her story was not told
very clearly, but the picture she painted was horrifying
enough. She took a deep breath.

"In Amsterdam," she began. "The tarts, the prostitutes
- you see - they sit in kind of shop windows. People

passing by see into lit-up little bourgeois bed sitters - chest of drawers, aspidistra, antimacassar - all in the window. The women smile and nod like this."

She forced herself to smile and in her distress the effect was grotesque. She nodded again. "Like this."

Tate moved. He protested, "Don't," but she was determined to finish. She therefore recovered herself enough to continue, suddenly loudly:

"Longman bought one, one night."

She turned to Tate then, to echo his false excuses. "Just a party, Tatty. Just the booze. Just one of those nights."

But Ramrod wanted accurate information. "You mean he bought this woman in front of you?"

"Oh, no! For God's sake." She laughed weakly. "He didn't buy her. That would have been too easy, too normal. He bought the room. The window. That's what he bought . . . For his wife." She shook her head furiously from side to side, trying to find control again. "To put me in it, don't you see?" Then control went altogether as she imitated a drunken Longman, calling the crowds with big beckoning gestures. "This way! This way! Walk up." She doubled forward for a moment and then cried, "You see the picture . . . the lewd cartoon." She looked down at her body, indicating it with her hands. "You see me, like this - imagine? . . . In the window, like this!"

Again she tried to make a joke of it, with a kind of wild, brittle self-hatred as if she wished she had not spoken at all. "Imagine!"

She stopped. They all seemed to hang in mid-air. She sat bolt upright on this rickety little bed, biting her lip furiously.

Then she broke.

19

"Oh glamorous night—" Annabelle said apprehensively. She had a small round face, and her brow crinkled up as she looked round Lab A. Longman had only put on two dim lights and there were deep blue shadows all around.

She touched the padding on the door and looked back at Longman who sat in his favourite spot, on the steps up to the gantry. She said, "Now here's a cheerful spot. This is surely the most sophisticated night club ever I saw." She had a strange little voice, rather husky and on one note. It was rather like a very smooth hovercraft, her voice, sliding along monotonously, refusing to be bounced up and down by the panic of the waves of emotion underneath. Already she was frankly frightened. Longman had drunk too much and was drinking more.

She raised her eyebrows and still looking round the room she asked, "What are we going to do? The imagination boggles. This is a site for rape, a cell for
. . ."

"Stop talking," Longman said and gestured with all the fingers of both hands. He even put the flask aside to beckon her over to him. Much more gently he said again, "Stop talking."

She came across slowly as she said, "I feel we must communicate - Perhaps it's this padded cell." Suddenly she called out. "Help!" There was no echo. "Help!" she yelled again, and the sound was muffled almost completely as it left her lips. She could hardly hear her own voice. "Oh dear," she said much more quietly, and stepping forward again she allowed him to slip his hands under her coat and pull her hips towards him. He stood up, then, and said:

"Communicate without speech."

But she did not want to be kissed. She shook her head. And in the same dotty, joking voice, she said:

"I really have to talk. 'Else I'll scream and scream."

Longman stepped away, made a wide gesture, a cartoon sweep of his arms.

"Fine. Scream - screams are good, and we won't disturb anybody. Make all the noises of love and they'll refuse to echo. It's a wonderful place. This is a modern trysting house." His mind seemed to wander again, for a few moments. "A trysting house for noisy couples."

Suddenly he ran up the steps and kicked the padding on the tank. "Sound-proof, echo-proof, sentiment-proof, highly original."

She stood at the bottom of the steps, looking up, with a deep frown.

He said, "You look like a golden spaniel puppy. Is your skin too loose?"

"Only in places," she said. "It fills out fine where I don't want it to." But she did not expect a laugh. She was merely playing the game of answering, her mind calculating whether it might not be better to run for it now.

Longman walked farther up the gantry, speaking loudly and cheerfully again.

"There's a bath here," he said, "should you care for extra treatment. We can have music too," he added, spotting the microphone. His face hardened. "Astonishing recordings. A great machine, miss, through here in Lab B: you can separate every instrument, and hear a symphony played on the bassoon."

He was silent for a moment, coming down the steps slowly, and she asked him very quietly:

"What's wrong? This isn't a party after all. I think I'm about to cry."

He put the palm of his hand against her cheek and

said, "It's soft," as if surprised, then he moved quite
quickly into Lab B. When she was about to follow he
told her firmly to stay exactly where she was. He
went farther. His demonstration would take a few moments
to prepare. He sat her down at the trestle table, and left
her with the remains of the flask, but she did not drink
anything. Longman himself seemed brisker, more sober
again.

She sat numbly while he pottered about in the little
lab next door. The doors were all open so she could
hear him humming and whistling "My darling Clementine". It must have taken him a quarter of an hour to
fix the speaker and tapes so that sound would be produced
in Lab A, not, as usual, in Lab B, alone. He worked steadily and happily as if he had quite forgotten her. But
just before he finished, as he connected something in
Lab A, he gave her a very friendly, nice, normal smile
and said, "Hello."

"Hello."

"I think you're very nice."

"I think I'm crazy. I'm meant to be giving a party
on a barge, not sitting on a hard wooden seat."

He smiled at her again, then disappeared into Lab
B. He closed the door behind him, switched on, and
spoke into the microphone.

In Lab A, Annabelle was surprised. The voice was
loud, in her ear.

"Ladies and gentlemen, Cabaret time in the Old
Tryst House. We proudly present man as Longman . . .
Longman screaming. Or if you prefer, Longman crying
as a boy, Longman sexy, very, very sexy, if that appeals.
All the noises of no love! Less rapturous than love,
that is, but altogether more sensual. I think that one
would be the most entertaining. Erotica in the trysting
lab. Are we ready? . . . Go."

The tape he switched on covered the end of the second
stage, leading from sensual distortions to animal panic.
Even without the echo it filled Lab A and magnified
like this, it terrified Annabelle. She was standing up,

stiffly, whitefaced, as Longman wandered back into Lab A, apparently amused, vaguely, by the sound of his own voice, from the tank. He came right up beside her, but did not look at her.

"You're not really weird?" she asked very meekly.

"Not a bit," he said cheerfully. "That's just a cabaret, night club titivation, to make your glands go faster. A mere demonstration of the sort of passions we bottle up. Everybody, my dear spaniel; you, too. Think what lies ahead."

Annabelle's crisp edge had gone. She spoke without facetiousness now.

"Please switch it off. If it's a joke, I really don't like it. If it isn't a joke then I think I'm scared out of my wits."

"But it is a joke —" he assured her. "It's the biggest, the greatest joke. All the yelling, all that, it just gives you an appetite for breakfast, that's all. And a desire to touch. Do you feel the need —"

"Please let's go away." She moved a little too quickly and he grabbed her.

"Don't run away."

"Please."

He was very strong and he pulled her hard against him as if he needed the pressure of her body against his, from head to knee. The tape was very loud at that moment, and her protests were in vain. But suddenly, a few seconds later, the noise of panic ceased and gave way to the sound, on the tape, of the water washing against the side of the tank and Longman's heavy breathing. Nothing else.

At once, he let go of her and his hands dropped to his sides. He was very pale, and apparently bewildered by his own action. Annabelle stood quite still. At last he turned away.

"Oh Lord," he said. "Oh Lord," and walked back to the steps, standing there for a moment, hanging on to the bannister, listening to the wash of the water, and the sound of his own sighs.

Annabelle was no coward. She did not run, now. Instead she said, "Why don't you switch that thing off?"

"Oh Lord," he said again.

She went across and took his hand.

"Tell me where, and I'll switch it off."

He shook his head. To get a better look at his face which seemed thin now, with a blue jowl, in this odd light, she sat on the step. No sooner had she done so, than he dropped on his knees and laid his head against her. Soon after, the noise of panic filled the room again, but Annabelle stayed where she was, frightened to move, running her hand again and again through his hair.

They were like this when the tape was suddenly switched off, some half an hour later. They did not move when the door burst open and Ramrod came in, followed by Oonagh. Tate was in Lab B. It was he who had switched off the tape.

Ramrod put on another light, then spotted the couple at the bottom of the steps.

"For God's sake," he asked Annabelle. "Are you all right?"

Flatly Annabelle answered, "Splendid." She looked quite washed-out.

Longman, without raising his head, indeed exactly as if he never wished to raise it from that lap, said, "Go away."

Annabelle, seeing Oonagh in the doorway now, tried to reintroduce a lighter note. But her face betrayed her, as usual. Poker-voiced, however, she said, "Berlin's night life has come to Oxford. All we need are some nude boys galloping round on white mares."

But Ramrod paid no attention to that. He tried to get Longman to pull himself together, but failed, so then he called Tate in. At last, slowly, Longman lifted his head and sat round. He assumed a fat smile as he saw his wife, and she stood quite still waiting for an insult. But it never came. Ramrod talked levelly and very seriously.

"Longman, I want you to listen carefully."

Longman sniffed and said, "In that case you'd better pass me my flask."

Ramrod hesitated, then decided to oblige him. Moving to the table for it, he turned to Oonagh and spoke to her in the same quiet manner.

"Please sit down. This is very serious, and very important to you. We are going to do something now which very clearly should have been done many weeks ago." He screwed the tap on the flask as he spoke, and handed it back to Longman who at once unscrewed it again. He said, "Tate is going to put on a tape."

"More noises —" Longman interrupted.

"A tape which neither Longman nor anyone else has played since the day we did our experiment this spring."

"Oh glorious day —"

Ramrod ignored Longman's haphazard interruption.

"On that tape you will hear your husband being interviewed by Doctor Tate and myself, a moment after we had taken him from the tank. This was the part of the experiment of which he had no foreknowledge."

Longman lowered his flask. He said, "The Major's barking up the wrong tree."

Ramrod continued, "This was a controlled experiment in which we used an old interrogation routine. Tate and myself playing sympathetic and unsympathetic questioners according to a pre-arranged plan. . . . When Longman hears this tape —"

Longman barked like a dog. But Ramrod continued, heavily, "— We believe that he will, if not at once, then very soon, find an explanation for some of the actions he has taken during the past weeks."

Again Longman barked. With a little laugh and a shake of his head he told his new friend Annabelle, "The wrong tree. . . . The Major is barking up the wrong tree."

"I don't think so," Ramrod said, then he instructed Tate to play the tape and he himself sat down at the table, next to Oonagh. When the tape had started, still with the noises of Longman being dragged from the

tank Tate too drifted back and sat by the table. He
was very shaky, looking no one in the eye. None of
them watched Longman whose reactions were now vital
to them. Aware of their attention, knowing them too
frightened to look him in the eye, he fidgeted a great
deal throughout, occasionally laying his hand on Annabelle's breast or on her thigh. She sat quite still,
concentrating hard, trying to understand what had twisted
the man beside her. Oonagh was like a cypher, betraying
no emotion. The tape recording was extremely clear.
All the nuances of friendship in Tate's voice were still
there. Listening to them even Longman, at last, settled
and was quiet.

Slowly they came to the noise of Longman's last
protest and his collapse across the table.

Tate's voice was much louder in their ears.

"Norman - for God's sake! Ambulance. . . ."

There were more sounds, then Tate's voice, "What
have you made me do?" A long pause, before the same
question. "Major, what have you made me do?"

Then the tape snapped. In the subsequent silence,
Tate went out to Lab B, switched off the machine. When
he returned the room was still. They were all frozen in
their places.

20

It was Annabelle who broke the silence at last. She
said simply, "I have the feeling that that tape will go
on playing at the end of the world," and Longman, very,

very, soberly touched her on the knee, smiled, and said,
"Good for Annabelle."

The monstrosity of the experiment had knocked the
life out of them all. Even Ramrod had lost his momentum,
as if for a few seconds the blinkers had dropped and
he was seeing for the first time the risk he had taken.
The cost was written straight across Oonagh's face.

It was therefore with urgent hope that they looked
towards Longman as he rose stiffly to his feet. He
certainly seemed more sober, cooler, more reasonable.
Oonagh leant forward trying to read his face, and the
plea in her own eyes made Tate bury his nails into
his palms as he clenched his fists. By now, he knew why.

Longman admitted, "I hadn't heard it, and it makes
peculiar listening. I've never heard you so helpful, Tatty."

Tate did not lift his eyes.

Ramrod, still with hope, asked, "You really listened?"

"I really listened," Longman said.

"Then you understand why you've been behaving
like this to your wife?"

Longman smiled; a sphinx of a smile, here.

"How have I behaved towards her, Major?"

"I think you know what I mean," Ramrod said nervously, glancing towards Oonagh who already seemed
to have heard something which the others had not recognized. She sat back, her face a dry mask again. Ramrod
continued. "It would be unnecessarily painful for both
of you . . ." He lost his way, then said, more definitely,
"For instance, this action of yours in the Amsterdam
red-light district."

Longman seemed delighted by the reference. He laughed
brightly.

"Oh, she told you that one did she? I bet she enjoyed
that. How much did you tell them, Otter? . . . Otter?"

But Oonagh did not answer.

Longman said lightly, "Did she add that nobody made
an offer? Not one Dutchman. Not one guilder was offered.
Tut, tut, tut, tut." He clicked his teeth, then grinned
again. "Major," he said equally brightly, "I told you.

You're barking up the wrong tree."

The others froze. Ramrod rose to his feet, horrified, now quite uncertain how to act. That the replay of the tapes should have no effect, except perhaps to strengthen Longman, in his new role, was something which had never occurred to the blinkered military man. Suddenly these questions of true responsibility, which more modest civilians consider daily, were there to be answered. They greatly confused him. It was almost as if one side of his face blushed while the other grew pale. He had no voice left. Speech stuck. And even if he had found his voice he would have had nothing to say before the club-man's astonished and horrified, "But this is unthinkable! This is not according to the rules! The Queen's regulations on spy-interrogations definitely state, sir, that tapes played back to brain-washed victims return victims to their previous lines of thought." Ramrod looked stunned and giddy. Tate was on the verge of tears.

Longman appeared to enjoy their reactions greatly. He was one up, so he felt, and told them so. "I'm very sorry, Major," he said with a laugh, then elaborated with a big, mocking gesture.

" 'Abracadabra' - no result. Not an inch off the launching pad. . . . 'Abracadabra,' the Major said, Major Svengali, but he hasn't pulled it off, the point being that even if I haven't heard the tapes, my dear guilt-ridden, con-science-struck sons, I remember damn well the whole questionnaire."

Tate found his voice. It came as a low and desperate whisper.

"But you're failing to understand. Longman, let it sink in. Don't you see, I was only acting the part of your friend - you don't understand - it was a put-up show. What I said was quite untrue . . . I was deliberately poisoning your mind."

"Of course I see that," Longman answered. "Just as I see why you agreed to the whole machiavellian scheme," he added slyly. "It never occurred to you that old Longman could be one ahead? Of course I understand.

The Major hasn't got the monopoly on mind bending in Curzon Street North, or wherever it is he practices." He looked pleasantly at Ramrod. "A kind of hangman, I suppose that's what you are. Hang 'em in the morning and a pint of bitter for lunch. Separate operations, not to be thought of, out of correct category?"

Ramrod did not answer, so Longman went on, "I twigged at the time, right at the time, as I sat at that table giving a very convincing picture of poor Jean Bonvoubois - whom I now greatly suspect - I sat, there, on that seat, and rumbled exactly what the pair of you were up to."

"Nonsense," Ramrod said.

"True," Longman flatly contradicted. "The only thing was that I was too exhausted to laugh. It seemed easier to play along. And I mean laugh, because there was very nice irony there." He paused. "Couldn't you see you were converting the converted?"

The horror of it crept up their spines. Here was the monster in Longman's clothing. And he kept laughing and joking.

"All that stuff about the feel of her, the smell of her . . . all that. D'you think that was news to me? Have you ever slept with her? . . ."

Oonagh was the only one who did not drop her head as he jeered her. "Not even the tart-searching Dutchman, not for a guilder." He turned back to Ramrod for a moment. "Did you think you had to tell me? Sons, I've slept with her." Slowly he paced over to where Oonagh sat. "I've even gone on sleeping with her, my eyes tight closed, my senses, smell, touch, the lot - cut off, imagining for all my worth any other woman - *any* - that's how married love was made!"

His voice had risen considerably. He shouted this last sally right into Oonagh's face and she did not flinch. Ramrod, hopelessly, thinly, said then, "You asked me once about the files we keep. I could find twenty people to testify that what you have just said is untrue. Every lecturer and student in Biology knew that you and Mrs.

Longman were the happiest couple in Oxford —"

"So we pretended —"

"I didn't," Oonagh said, and it was like a shot in the dark. There was no throb in the voice, no self-pity, no hidden tears. It was fact and rang as fact. Longman made an elaborate, facetious bow. He behaved like a liar, and convinced only one person of his lies - himself.

"Then let's say *I* pretended, Otter dear. I sometimes even bluffed myself. Those midnight picnics, what about that? . . . The big stuff . . . *Amour, amour, amour.* There's the picture of the husband really keeping up the bluff."

"No," Oonagh said, fact again. Simply "No" meaning "I know for certain that this is untrue" and her conviction enraged him for a moment. He quite lost control and yelled back at her.

"God damn it, woman, I know! I'm talking about myself! Me!" For a moment he looked as if he would hit her, then he seemed to decide against it. He turned away.

"Oh, for Christ's sake," he said, much quieter again. "Why not accept that your little experiment didn't work. Except to make me live a long time in a single afternoon. That's the only effect. So I come a little quicker to the conclusion which is inevitable and maybe we should be grateful for that. It saves the analyst's bills. Here we are, in one step. . . . The point of truth!" He raised his flask and toasted Oonagh before he drained it. "The party's over now . . ."

Oonagh was unshakeable; very calm, serious, even set. Quietly but as firmly as before she answered him then:

"I love you and we have not come to the point of truth, I promise."

Longman looked at her as if she were at the other end of a powerful reversed telescope; a tiny, distant figure.

"More midnight picnics, *cherie*? Forty days and forty nights?"

"No," she replied sensibly. "That's not what I'm thinking about at all. That affair was a journey from a firm base, and if it was a dangerous one that was perhaps as much my fault as the fault of your early experiments. I wanted you too much. But it was only a journey, for the firm base was - and is - a love that has lasted fourteen years." She said, without pride, it seemed, but again with factual conviction, "That love is indestructible."

It was Annabelle who broke, not Oonagh. It was she who could not stand the cruelty of Longman's reaction; his shrug and his "huh!". She rushed from the room, unable to sit and witness more. At once, Longman rushed after her, shouting, "Hey!" and "Wait!" Yelling, "Hey there, Annabelle!"

He caught up with her outside the lab as she stumbled on the edge of the lawn in the half dark.

She said, "Let me go, please. I don't want anything to do with this! I've had enough, enough of awfulness without all this creepy sick stuff. Please leave me alone. I'd rather go alone."

The sight of her genuine distress seemed to have a curious effect on Longman. He answered in a voice she scarcely recognized.

"You're running away," he said, and seemed himself surprised. There was tenderness: more, a kind of tender desperation in his voice.

Annabelle stood quite still, for a second, staring at him.

"What *are* you, anyway?" she asked, and answered herself. "It's not exactly hollow. You're a kind of echo of a man."

Longman paused, then after a second the effort of self-rescue seemed too great. He threw his chance away, and spoke ironically again.

"I told you, my wife doesn't understand me . . . Only that's serious." He smiled in a forced sort of way. "Come on, run you back. You can't walk, anyway. I promise, no dramatics."

She looked at him sideways, and went with him half in bewilderment, half in fear. But man's not unattractive like that.

They went in the Lagonda, followed, of course, by our man Ramrod, driving Tate's car, with headlights dipped.

21

How much the Jekyll and how little the Hyde there was in Longman at this time it is impossible to say. Apart from anything else, he had drunk considerably and he seemed to be varying between complete sobriety at one moment, and hectic drunkenness at the next. He drove very fast and dangerously over the meadow to the barges, but when he switched off the car engine he looked perfectly sober.

But Annabelle had had enough. At once she opened the car door to get out. Longman caught her by the wrist and she was frightened by his intensity again, as he said, "Let me come."

Recovering herself as best she could she seemed to decide to treat him like any other drunken, amorous male. She had met enough of these; frustrated students and wolves in mortar boards. She pulled his hand from her wrist without difficulty and replaced it on his lap.

"You're going home to bed, alone."

He shook his head. At this moment he was serious and cold, almost frightened himself. He asked her for a cigarette and, reluctantly, she provided one. He began, "I want to talk, I—"

"Stop," Annabelle said at once.

Almost shyly Longman said, "I won't be violent, I promise."

But Annabelle still did not want to hear. She simply said, "No," meaning "No" to all or any of his stories.

"No joke. I'm pushed."

"I won't listen, professor," she said in a low voice, and he frowned. "I don't want to hear. I'm not going to bore you with the complicated people that have bashed and bruised my life. If I were charitable I suppose I might bend an ear, but a year or two ago Annabelle bought herself that barge there and opted to give charity the boot."

Longman still looked at his fingers on the steering wheel as he said, "I find you very attractive, I think that's all I have to say," and there was a little pause.

"That's it," she said with a firm nod, and prepared to leave the car. "I'm attractive - and I have every limb and organ a girl should have, except one. I no longer have a shoulder to weep on. A Polish gentleman wore that away with his tears." She leant across and kissed him, a quick peck on his lips and he did not now try to stop her.

As they had talked, a big black labrador on the prowl had stopped to look at them. It was a stupid, friendly dog that had called at the barges before and it sat looking at Annabelle as she was about to step on to the gang plank. Its tail wagged with a thump on the wet grass. Annabelle stopped and looked at it. Her frown was not unlike its own expression. She told it very slowly:

"Go away you dreadful, big, sad dog. You remind me of man." And then she vanished inside the old barge.

After a while Longman got out of the car and looked at the dying embers of the bonfire. The whole place still smelt acrid from the fireworks that the students had let off, but everybody had disappeared. Everybody, that is, except the dog that should have been called a hound. It whined with pleasure and excitement as Longman started to walk slowly down the towpath, putting his coat round him, buttoning up. It was colder away from the barges.

At last he stopped and sat on the grass by the river. The dog expected something of him, perhaps that he should throw in a stick, and alternately whined, barked, and wagged its tail delightedly. At last Longman paid attention to it and invited it closer. It came up to be patted and put a paw on his knee, but Longman still did not touch it. Instead, he looked into its face and said:

"Moosh, don't look so trustingly at me. You are just a series of conditioned reflexes, not a dog at all. You're a Pavlov puppet, nothing more. We could take you to Biology, alas, poor baffled moosh, and train you there. Every time we ring a bell, you'll bark, ring two, your mouth will water, ring three and you'll howl for sex."

The dog whined and he patted it at last.

"Machine in furry clothing," he called it then, and it barked. "Hark, hark, the dogs do bark, the biologist's coming to town. Get thee to a widow with a cupboard and a bone, or they'll get you, dog. They'll get you and bend your apology for a mind. They can do it, moosh, they can. Believe poor baffled man."

22

Still in Lab A, waiting for Ramrod's return, Oonagh told Tate, "Hall shouldn't have bothered to follow. Longman won't harm her. He won't hurt any other woman. He never did."

"Oonagh, don't be so calm." Then, as if to ask her something else, he followed her from the table over to the window where she had opened the shutters, and was staring at the big lab opposite. The concrete shone white in the moonlight. There seemed to be nobody within miles, and Tate had lost his voice.

At last, she asked, "What are you really saying, Tate?" and she sounded quite severe. Even the tone of her voice, however, could not prevent him now. There was no question of him seizing her. He never would have dared do that. But as if his head had grown too heavy for him he let it drop until his mouth could feel the down on her forearm, which was exposed, as she still held on to the shutter. Very gently he kissed her skin.

She said, "You baby."

Tate blushed, then came to his senses. He said, "I swear it's only since I've seen you hurt —"

But she was very firm with him now. Only just controlling her anger, she said, "Don't lie."

"I swear that's true," he lied again. "I didn't know last summer. If I had I'd never have agreed to the experiment. I promise. It was only tonight when I saw you on the barge. At the earliest," he claimed, "when I saw you at your own house . . . I knew how much I'd misled you then. And it frightened me. I didn't know before then. . . . Oonagh, nobody can be blamed for falling in love."

She did not turn away from the window as she said again, "You are a baby - a baby!"

Tate was in tears. His weakness was almost horrifying.

"Oonagh, please believe me, I'd do anything for you."

Still she did not answer, but wandered back to her chair by the table and sat down, waiting for Ramrod's return. There was a long protracted silence while Tate stood frozenly staring at her. Then he too sat down and started digging his nail into the soft wood of the trestle table. Minutes later he said:

"I promise I didn't know *consciously*." She did not say anything even then, so he said it all for her. His self-hatred was almost less attractive than his childishness.

"It makes it worse, doesn't it?" he asked the statue opposite. "I can't even recognize my own motives. That's real ignorance. I hate that sort of person. What can I say?"

She did not prompt him, and he stood up again and paced about. It seemed hours to them both before Ramrod returned to report that the pair had arrived safely at the barges. Oonagh collected her handbag and prepared to leave. Tate did not dare offer to run her home. Ramrod, surprised by Tate's hesitation, suggested he might do so but got the reply:

"No, thank you."

Ramrod said, "Mrs. Longman, you are looking very tired now. I honestly don't think you should walk home alone. Not all the way to Tackley Place."

"It isn't far."

"You wouldn't think of going to the barges?"

She did not reply. Ramrod took a step forward to make his point more strongly. "You mustn't consider that. It could be very dangerous."

She said flatly, "He's come near enough to murder before. Why should it be more dangerous tonight?"

"It could be," Ramrod said. "I'd rather you didn't risk it."

At that, for a moment, her strength returned, and she said, "It isn't such a risk when you think that I'd rather be killed by him than live without him. But it won't happen. He'll come back. That much I know. There's something - some instincts in Longman, as in everybody else, that are indestructible, no matter what you or Tate or Science can do to him. Of that I am sure."

She turned to leave and when Ramrod tried to restrain her again she said very coldly:

"Leave me be. I'd rather go alone."

All of an hour later she came on Longman who was still playing with the dog. He was muttering to it as it fetched him a stick.

"Fetch and carry. How de-you-do. Dog, I love thee not . . ." Then out of the corner of his eye he spotted Oonagh's approach. She could hear him quite clearly when he told the dog:

"Don't look now, thing. Nanny's here." The dog barked and wagged its tail as it bounded forward and Oonagh patted it. At last she asked Longman:

"May I sit here, too?"

He was leaning his back on his elbows and staring into the inky water. He did not even glance over his shoulder as he replied, "That's a matter between you and the Thames Conservancy Board . . . How did you get here?"

"I walked."

Longman stretched his legs out.

"You horrible, brave little thing. You remind me of a war widow selling red cross flags on a cold afternoon."

Oonagh sat down beside him all the same.

She said, "If you want to kill me, you only have to push," and he did not reply. She was staring at him and he did not like her scrutiny. At last she said, "I love you - God knows where you are."

At once he jumped to his feet, saying, "Oh, for crying

out loud," and when the dog barked loudly, he cried, "Hark, hark, the dogs do bark, the nannies are coming to town." He walked away very swiftly towards the car and the barges which must have been nearly a quarter of a mile downstream. Oonagh followed, distractedly. Her strength and pride had collapsed all at once. She cried imploringly, "Wait for me. Please wait. Longman, please —"

Very suddenly he stopped on the towpath, turned round and looked at the crouched figure shuffling after him. "Why should I wait?"

"It's - it's slippery," she said, and that was true. "Don't go too fast. Please wait."

She reached out a hand towards him and after a second's hesitation he grabbed it, behaving now like a bad-tempered urchin with an unwanted sister. Roughly, then, he pulled her forward and started walking at an absurdly fast pace which she could not possibly keep up with. Alice, she was, dragged by the Red Queen. For a moment she managed to keep her feet somehow, stumbling along, crying now, with the dog bounding beside her barking all the time. Above the noise of the barking, Longman was shouting:

"Come on, then, come on! Back to the love nest."

Breathlessly, nearly screaming, Oonagh begged him to slow up at least. "Oh, stop. Please stop." Then at last, inevitably she fell on her knees, and still he dragged her until her knee cracked a stone embedded in the mud and she fell then flat on her face, grazing her cheek against the cinders on the path. In great pain she lay there, almost too weak to sob. She did not even lift her head as the dog came close and snuffled round her face and whined.

Longman asked clearly, "Are you going to get up, or do I have to lift you?"

"I can't —" she said faintly.

"What's the matter with you?" His voice carried to the other side of the stream and seemed to echo on some willows there, but Oonagh's pain was in the body now, heavy and serious. Her cheek was still on the ground as she asked, hopelessly:

"Can't you remember? Oh God Almighty, isn't it yours, too?"

Longman stood quite still, frowning. The dog went to Oonagh again and she said, "Dog, please go away." It licked her face, but still she did not lift it. Without bending down to her, but not so loudly now, Longman asked:

"Is the child coming? . . . Don't just weep! Answer!"

Oonagh raised her head for a second.

"I don't know."

"Of course you know," he said, but his face betrayed his voice. He looked confused while he spoke clearly. "Think."

But Oonagh only answered, weakly, "I don't care. I don't care." Then she closed her eyes.

23

Annabelle was asleep when he kicked on the door, insistently, yelling for her at the top of his voice. But waking, she soon recognized who it was.

She said, "Push off. I'm asleep."

"For God's sake, girl —"

"Yankee, go home."

"Annabelle, I need help."

"I told you."

"I'm with Oonagh. Open up."

Annabelle moved from her bed, asking with less

conviction now. "Who's kidding?" Then she opened
up.

Longman practically fell through the door. He had
carried his wife the whole way. He managed to say,
"Try and take some of the weight," as he ducked his
head to get through, and together, clumsily, they put
her on the bed. The cabin was in a chaotic mess, with
glasses and plates everywhere. Oonagh closed her eyes
as soon as she lay on the bed and appeared to pass
out.

Immediately following an explosion or an accident,
when the debris and the carnage lie about us, while we
ourselves remain unhurt, we are left for a moment without
feeling and without thought. The shock is too great for
us, and we do not cope at all. So it seemed to be with
Longman now.

Annabelle had to ask him several times, louder and
louder, "What happened?" before he moved. He took
a step along the side of the bed and looked at his wife's
bruised face. "She fell," he said, non-committally, and
Annabelle almost cringed away from him, horrified by
his callousness. Then a quick cloud passed across his
face. He said, "I pushed her, I suppose. I forgot about
the child." He shook his head. "We've got to do something." But he was incapable of decision. The dog,
somehow, had got into the cabin and he first turned
on it, shooing it out and calling it a tramp. Then he
went over to his wife and put his hand on her shoulder
where her thin coat was torn, and in a way quite unlike
himself, in a paternal way, almost the family doctor's
professional way, he said, "You'll be all right. It'll
be okay. Sure it will." Very slowly then he took his
own coat off and rolled up his sleeves.

Annabelle said everything in whispers. She asked,
"Is the baby coming?"

Longman answered, "Yep," almost uncommittedly.
"Where's your phone?"

When she said, "I haven't one," he almost laughed,
holding the bridge of his nose between finger and thumb.

"There wouldn't be one on Tate's barge?"

She shook her head and now he did laugh, weakly, then looked round him angrily, as if to say, "This is a trap . . . I'm trapped, I've been conned into this."

Annabelle suggested: "There's a box about a mile upstream by the footbridge."

Longman seemed glad about this. He started to roll down his sleeve again, saying, "I'll take the car."

But Oonagh reached out and clutched him, with both hands, shouting loudly, "No."

Longman was surprised by the vigour of the gesture. Still looking at his wife he asked Annabelle, "Can you drive?"

But Annabelle's "No, I'm afraid not," was almost drowned by Oonagh's shouting.

"If you go, I'll die. I'll die! I know I will. I know these things. Longman stay, don't you see? You must stay!"

She finished abruptly as a bad contraction gripped her whole body and her back, passing like a low, hammer cramp down to the very base of her spine. She was sitting up awkwardly clutching on to Longman when the pain took her by surprise. Instead of knocking her back on to the bed, the spasm had a curious effect. In trying to relieve the intense pain she reared up, holding Longman's shoulder, and she let out a strange, frail cry. Longman held her, his face a mask, his hands doing the right thing, supporting her round shoulder and breast. Gradually the pain eased.

He asked, "Still hurt?" as he held her, then gently let her back on to the bed. "D'you think that pain's normal?"

She answered strangely. "Not if you stay. . . . No pain," and closed her eyes again.

Annabelle was conscious mainly of her own inadequacy. The situation for her seemed to be a baffling and frightening conclusion to the most baffling evening of her life. She knew, perhaps, less of life than she liked to pretend. She had never taken part in a birth, never seen death. She moved her hands wildly as if she were making a cat's cradle, and then suggested, "I'll run to the phone. It won't take long."

"Get a few things first," Longman said, then he broke off. Oonagh was still clinging to his arms, preventing him from moving away. He told her firmly, "Oonagh, you must let go. Let go of me."

Oonagh said, "Stay. Promise?" still holding on.

More gently, at last, he answered, "I promise I'll stay."

His behaviour at this stage was curiously professional. He seemed very stable beside Oonagh, now. He was like a doctor whose patient was too fond of him. He did not rebuke her for her affection but did his best to suppress it. This act of suppression had a depth to it, as if all the time - and he seldom took his eyes off her - he was struggling to understand why she should love him and why he should feel it necessary to reject the idea of loving her back. This iota of change already made a difference to Oonagh. Her eyes seemed enormous, but there was hope in them. The blue veins behind the white skin of her exposed neck when she lay with her head right back made her look more than ever vulnerable and frail.

Annabelle asked, "Do I boil kettles?" and Longman again seemed to try and rid himself of his own thoughts and turn to action.

"What the hell for?" he asked.

Annabelle shrugged. "Well, I don't know," she said. "I just heard. . . ."

Longman shook his head. "I never know what they do with all that boiling water. You'd better give me some sheets and —" He looked round the dirty plates, the piled olives and sardines, the empty bottles of tonic, the ashtrays filled with stubbed-out cigarettes. "Have you any disinfectant?"

Annabelle was pleased to be of help at last. "Yes, I have."

Longman muttered, "There are rules about hygiene. Get the sheets and disinfectant then hop it and ring the nearest witch-doctor."

The lightness of his voice was encouraging. He seemed capable of action for the first time and he turned back quickly to hold Oonagh's hands very tight as her body arched with the next contraction. The pain seemed to be very bad. She was in a worrying state of exhaustion to be starting on a birth. These clinical facts impressed themselves on Longman's mind, at last, and concentrating on them he seemed to forget, at least for the moment, the confusion within him. Asking about the contractions he said, "Often?" and she nodded. He said seriously and rightly, "Good." He did not want the first period to be protracted to any great length of time. That would take too much out of her for her to manage the birth herself.

It was not that he was speaking to her with natural affection. The sympathy he gave still had this professional air. But he seemed to be happier in himself - the lab man re-employed. He was thinking ahead about the experiment alone, occasionally humming a bar or two as he moved the worst of the debris from the scene of the action. Nor did he forget to comfort the patient. Her strength was an essential factor to the success of the experiment. Her contractions came with increasing frequency. He said, "That's right and proper. I remember the textbook." Not long after, he looked at her and considered. She was coping with the pains better, but she was still arching on her back and he decided to change her position. He gestured and said, by way of instruction, "On one side," then he helped her, pushing her over very gently with one hand, the other flat on the front of her shoulder acting as a safe brake. So she turned gently. He managed then to take her coat off and undoing her dress at the back, he found he could slip his hands through and massage her back. He did so with firm movement, patiently, and almost in time with those long-fingered strokes, he told her a little joke.

He said quietly, "I've always fancied the osteopath's racket. . . . I knew one, once. . . . But he was a bit free with his hands. A fat debutante's mother - the mother being thin, of course, thin as a horse - she had

him struck off . . . 'Altogether too much temptation'
. . . my friend said in court. 'She was fifteen stones I
guess.' "

Her face was away from him, but she nodded, acknowl-
edging his joke. She had recovered wonderfully well,
already. There were no tears now. The same firmness
that was the very core of Oonagh had returned. Her
face was pale and determined, her eyes extraordinarily
bright, her hair already a little damp above the dirty
mark of the cinders and the mud, the bruise and mat
of blood.

Annabelle came back into the cabin clumsily like
a schoolgirl excitedly setting out on a girl's camping
expedition. She brought the linen and the Milton.

"Is that all?" she asked.

Longman did not move from the bed where he still
sat massaging Oonagh's back. He looked over his shoulder
and checked.

"That's all," he said. "You can tell the witch-doctor,
when you get him on the line, that I reckon we're almost
at the end of the first stage."

Annabelle looked blank. "What does that mean?"

"That's what I like about English girls' education,"
he replied. "You better go quick."

She paused, then nodded violently and left the cabin.
But at the door she paused, then stuck her head in
again.

"Is it all right?"

Longman did not look as confident as he sounded
but neither of the girls saw his face. He said, "Fine,
honey. She's no beginner. She's done it before," and
putting his hand round the thin neck beneath him, he
added, "She'll do it again."

Then Annabelle closed the door. As she ran across
the upper deck her footsteps sounded very loud. But
just before she stepped ashore Longman called out to
her again.

"Yes?" she called back.

He said, "Scissors."

"God," she said.

"It's all right. I'm only clearing decks."

"I meant 'God, I'm not sure where they are'." Then suddenly she remembered.

"Yes, on the dressing table. Behind the mirror with a lot of other muck."

"Fine," he said, then he dismissed her again and she ran off. In the cabin they could hear the dog bark.

"Hark, hark," Longman murmured as he moved over to the dressing table and was amazed at what an understatement she had made. Behind the mirror lay a whole barber's shop of curlers, scents, powder, combs, and at last, scissors.

Outside Annabelle was saying to the dog, "No? Not cheerful now." As she ran up the towpath she muttered, "Dog, for heaven's sake."

Longman knew the patient was too weak to stand up, or even sit up and remove her clothes. That is why he took the scissors. As he began to cut down the side of her dress he said, "I've often wanted to do this," but she did not react. She seemed to be very quiet and frighteningly weak. But she knew how to reserve every ounce of strength. Still massaging her, a quarter of an hour later, he said, "I know what I'm doing, woman. . . . Child. Don't worry. Anyway, you can shout if there's anything I forget."

24

The first stage took longer than Longman had feared. It seemed to run on, interminably, the contractions as sharp and frequent as before. She said, "It just goes *on*," and Longman said, "Sh."

He was warm himself now, getting down to serious work, tearing the sheets in half. Many things he said now, and had said over the past half hour, were humorous, but he felt far from happy. He was not smiling himself.

The legs of the extraordinary folding bunk were sagging, and he kicked them straighter, looking for the first time at the complications of the contraption. He sounded surprised.

He said, "This damn thing's collapsible. It only needs me to put my flat foot on the wrong strut and you'll be the first woman to have a baby on her head."

"It just goes *on* —" she said again.

"It won't be long now."

"Is something wrong?" She sounded frightened now and the pain seemed to shake her whole body.

"Not a thing. Nothing's wrong." His voice was firm. A sedative would have been a help. He said, "It's only a pity that Annabelle isn't a dope fiend." Then he added, "And rather a surprise, I suppose." Soon, he moved back to her side, took her hand, and gripped her hand when the worst waves of pain broke and shuddered her. She was like too small a yacht now, adrift in heavy seas. But he held on to her, assuring and re-assuring her, all the time. There was still no sign of Annabelle.

"Easy as you can," he said. "We'll need all the energy over the brow."

He had prepared a hot drink. Chocolate, fairly typically, was the only thing Annabelle kept in that line. Making her sip a little, in a moment freer from pain, he remarked, "It's odd, this. I've never conducted the oldest physiological experiment in the world." Then he put the mug aside.

He said, "Come on, now, let's try this breathing stunt they're always arguing about on woman's pages."

Longman would have made a superb clinician. This was clear now. He was almost hypnotizing her as he conducted her breaths. She took a long in-breath, and then watching her body carefully, he told her when to let out each little gasp. "Now, now, short, short breath

out. . . . All out. . . . And in again, big, big breath.
Hold. . . . Now out, short, short out, out. . . ." They
went on a while like this with great success. So much
success that he smiled for the first time. "Not bad,"
he said, "I believe it helps," and then holding her hands
he found he could guide her more closely by feeling
the tightness of her grip. She reacted well to him, but
said nothing, her mind on one objective, one only now.
"Adam and Eve stuff," Longman said as she breathed
deep in again.

Only once she tried to speak. She was going to tell
him she loved him, to ask him something more. But
he would not allow it. He wanted her concentration complete.

"Don't dare talk," he said gently, and then he realized
that they were passing into the second stage. He interrupted
to ask "Yes?" and she nodded, "Yes, I think so."

As he pulled the covering sheet off her legs he said
again, "Don't talk, don't dare, or we'll clock you one
and haul him out with the tongs. Then you'd be sorry."

In her excitement, which was growing now, she laughed
a little. It came out strangely, her laughter, almost childishly, as it often does when someone is conquering pain.

He said, "I do believe you're getting excited."

"Yes."

She was about to shift but he restrained her, holding
her knee.

"No, don't move." He considered her position very
seriously, and used his brain. He murmured, "I don't
care what all the physicians have told you. We'll have
you stay right where you are, on your back, for a while.
That's where the story started, that's where it ends.
. . . Forget the text books," he added as he began now
to feel for the infant, "they're probably written by vets."

It was only a moment later when he said, "We're
getting places now, my friend. Oh, yes we are. But
not too fast or we'll be in trouble. No cuts, no stitches,
no panic, no carelessness. Think, Oonagh, concentrate!
think! listen! Clench your fists, hang on to the bed there

and do *not* shove. . . ." He was sweating profusely himself now, afraid that in her tiredness she would shove too quickly and too hard in order to finish the business quickly. On her fifth child she did not have too strong muscles for the essential, controlling, braking action. A birth, even at this last stage, should be a gradual thing, not an explosion.

"Hold, hold, hold . . ." he said, and steadied her again. "Come on, love," he persuaded her, "don't fail us now. . . . Very good." She was back under his control, thinking, working to plan. "Good. A little shove. A little more."

She was panting very hard and high now, feeling (as she had felt for the last half hour) that she could not manage another moment more.

"Brakes, brakes, brakes! Don't push for a moment. Don't."

She moaned.

"Hold it, love."

Between breaths she asked, "Can you see him yet?"

Longman himself was working hard to ease the baby's head through the last circle, without tearing tissue. He said, almost absently,

"You're all right. . . . Okay, okay, push a little. We're all clear and set. More push. You're very good! . . ." And then again there was a minor alarm, and he worked hard to free the child. "Easy, easy does it."

The head was almost through. The last moments were of furious activity, as the body was to follow. The whole business accelerated very suddenly and in this flurry of activity, Oonagh was half laughing and half crying. Her knee knocked against Longman's eye.

"For God's sake," he had time to shout, "don't knock the man out! Can you pull yourself up a little. . . . Up the bed?" His legs crashed against the ironwork, bruising him. She tried valiantly to move up a little, asking him, with desperate excitement now, "Is he there? Is he there?"

"Don't move or we'll ruin everything."

Suddenly, in the last second, some terrible fear seemed to strike her.

"Longman!" she yelled. But a second later, hers was not the only cry. Pouring with sweat, half over-balancing, Longman had the child in his hands, slippery, shiny, minute, bright red and blue, but whole, alive, in one piece. Longman, himself, was near panic now.

"For God's sake, what the hell do we do now? Can you remember how fast they cope with his problems?"

"Tie it now," she said, and her head was flat back on the pillow. "Tie twice."

As he worked, he said with a little bubble of excitement, "Scouting for boys," then he laid the baby still with its cord, on a pad at the end of the bed.

He now addressed it, firmly, saying, "You stay here for a second, my friend. . . . My friend that's born on a barge . . . for what, this time? . . . Pedro the fisherman, you'd better be."

Oonagh said, clear as a bell, "Longman?" But she hardly had the strength to pick up the rubber hot water bottle that had comforted her. He took it, at once, understanding, and put it by the child.

"Every comfort," he said, and only a moment later, Annabelle returned. Longman said to her, almost lazily, "Just in time, dear Annabelle. Get every dirty linen basket and box or we'll be had up for murder. And go and tear Tate's sheets from his bunk."

Poor Annabelle did not seem quite sure whether it was good news or bad. She saw the baby still on the bed and the two exhausted parents. Longman read her face. "Good news," he said, and at once she obeyed and ran over to the other barge, which was still empty.

The afterbirth is a terrible insult. The pain comes again. Helping Oonagh, Longman said, "We'll really have to get on to this one, in the labs." He massaged her tummy, steadily.

"Longman," she dared ask at last, "is it just as a doctor? Are you just the doctor?"

Longman paused. He did not seem confused or amazed.

Himself, he seemed to find it quite natural that he was back where he started, as her husband. It was as if a nightmare was over. He did not want to explain or examine it; merely to accept.

He said, "If I am, there's going to be more strikings off the list."

She reached up and touched the moisture on his cheeks.

She asked: "That's not all sweat?"

"No, darling, not all." Then he started work again. "Come on. Let's finish off."

25

Except with dying horses, Majors shall not blub. It's in the book. The ruling is perfectly clear. In spite, therefore, of Annabelle's tearful effusions, Ramrod had dry eyes. There was a job to complete - "follow through!" - "place cut-off gun!" - and complete it Ramrod would.

Annabelle was on the barge with Ramrod and Longman. The witch-doctor had already visited and done the essential - namely, fill in the birth form. Annabelle kept talking and talking as if she had shed fifteen years.

She said, "I could cry for a week. I think it's wonderful - wonderful, unqualified. Maybe I'm getting too old or too spinster, but I just want to laugh and cry for a week." Then, at last, taking Ramrod's raised bowler for the hint it definitely was, she disappeared below decks.

Ramrod naturally observed Longman with some care, but Longman smiled.

"I know what's going on inside that head of yours —"

"My dear sir, I assure you —"

"I know. But have a little faith, Major, I've come out all right. And if you'd please note, I have proved a point, even if at high cost. I refer to your filing system." He said, "You know now what immersion in that tank can do for a man and it's clear what it did for Sharpey. When he met those snow-booted characters they only had to tell him what to do. And Z for Zombie, not S for Sharpey, obeyed them and did it."

Majors should never acknowledge defeat, but Ramrod went so far as to admit that Longman could be correct. Then, as they set off down the towpath back to the town, he made one of those self disparaging yet still cheerful remarks which have enabled majors to lose millions of men, but no face. "Well, well," he said, "all's well that ends well" - a remark usually attributed to political thinkers on the other side. He added, "And let's face it, we've muddled through."

But Longman was not listening to him. He had that strange little song in his heart which we have when we escape gaol or come back from school or first come through sickness. It is simply an appreciation of everything around us - "Oh, you trees, oh, you sky, oh, you Christchurch Meadow - you." For Oonagh had said that there were instincts in man laid too deep for the most skilful mind-bender to probe. On that premise hangs this tale. And it had better be valid, not only for my sake, but yours, as well.

Other Bestselling SIGNET Fiction

SHIP OF FOOLS *by Katherine Anne Porter*
The big bestseller by one of America's most distinguished literary figures, in which an ocean voyage becomes a microcosm of life itself.   (#Q2333—95¢)

THE GARDEN *by Yves Berger*
The prize-winning novel of a young man's obsession and of the shocking crime that jolts him into reality.
                                                     (#P2489—60¢)

A CHARMED LIFE *by Mary McCarthy*
A worldly, vivid novel about the inhabitants of an artist's colony in a bleak New England seacoast town. By the celebrated author of *The Group*.   (#T2416—75¢)

INVISIBLE MAN *by Ralph Ellison*
A novel of extraordinary power about a desperate man's search for his identity. Winner of the National Book Award.
                                                     (#T1823—75¢)

'68 *by Peter Scaevola*
This powerful political novel projects into the near future when a dangerous demagogue manipulates American hate groups and is swept into the Presidency of the United States.   (#T2503—75¢)

ON THE BEACH *by Nevil Shute*
The gripping bestseller about men and women bravely facing inevitable extinction.   (#P2279—60¢)

THE MANCHURIAN CANDIDATE *by Richard Condon*
A Korean War hero is brainwashed and made the agent of a group of political assassins.   (#T1826—75¢)

To Our Readers: We welcome your request for our free catalog of SIGNET and MENTOR Books. If your dealer does not have the books you want, you may order them by mail, enclosing the list price plus 5¢ a copy to cover mailing. The New American Library of World Literature, Inc., P. O. Box 2310, Grand Central Station, New York, New York, 10017.